LASTVIEW

CANDACE TAYLOR JOHNSON

LASTVIEW IS A WORK OF LITERARY FICTION
The places, names of characters, events, mechanics, and incidents are used fictitiously or are a product of a very active imagination. Any resemblance to actual events is merely coincidental. Welcome to the world of Crime Fiction. So, sit back, or stand with humor. Buckle your reading belt and read LASTVIEW.

ISBN 978-0692385821

LASTVIEW
Author Candace Taylor Johnson
Lay-out Design by www.thefastfingers.com
Edited by Kerry Genova writerresourceinc.com
Cover Artist TheCoverCollection.com
E-mail Candacetj@gmail.com
Twitter @KnackTime

I dedicate this novel Lastview to readers and writers everywhere.

Thank you for your compassion of the Literary Arts.

Table of Contents

Chapter 1

That Dream Teal Always Have.

Rolling over once in a comfortable bed on an early warm morning, that dream Teal always have just before the alarm clock rings. She is holding her with blood on her hands an uniform. The service weapon is on the ground. Officer Wills is the first to arrive to the scene where he investigates the area and building at the Zoo. Teal can hear him on his radio say. "Four people down, two are fatal send an ambulance, and I need some back up now. There are two men lying in the street with gunshot wounds, and they are barely hanging on to life, and it is a man in the building then a female officer down too, hurry please. Teal, let her go!" She cried, "Wills, I'll never let her go I can't now she was driving the car! I told her to stop, but she brought us here." I can't believe you two girls are out here with no back up, and any bulletproof vest on. You're not supposed to be out here in this area, now look at this pitiful mess."

"Why did she bring you here?" Teal can hardly see the scene, or hear his question, as it faded with the loud sirens of the police car, also the noise of the ambulance arriving along with glaring red, and white lights flashing. Finally back up has arrived at the area. Wills partner Oren appears yelling!

"What happen Wills?"

"Look at the two of them lying over there in the street, and there's another one inside the building. He didn't make it. They're better off dead, but Brittany I'm so sorry."

"What are you talking about Brittany? Where is she?" Oren asked.

Wills pleaded, "No Oren you don't want to see this mess!"

Right away Wills is trying to guard Oren and protect him from the horrific scene. Oren shoved Wills to the side, and in shock he dropped to his knees next to her holding Brittany on the smeared splattered pavement, in a puddle of fresh blood, covering the ground, running down onto the sidewalk, dripping into the street with Oren screaming, "No Brittany, Teal!"

"What happen?"

"What happened to her?"

"What are the two of you doing out here?"

"Who did this?"

Teal responded, "She brought us here."

Ring! Then the sound of the alarm clock.

She awakens, rolls over, then shuts it off.

"That is the dream Teal always have War."

"Brently my son time to rise and stretch then get ready for school."

Brently is her six-year-old son. Calm, relaxed, and smart for his age she calls him Brent for a nickname. "First, I will fix you some hot cereal and, your uniform is ready with your socks and shoes. I'll get your clothes. Good job, you ate all your cereal. Time to go to the bathroom and get dressed. Don't forget that later your father will pick you up after school." Brent smiles because he loves his dad. He is finished dressing now there is the sound of the doorbell! I pressed the button to open the door which is an elevator leading up to my apartment. "Good morning." It's Tasha, and her daughter Angela. Tasha is Teal's sister a law enforcement officer that has settled working behind the desk. She is a caring person, five feet seven inches in height; honey colored skin, black hair and brown eyes.

"Is Brently ready?"

"Yes, and his father will pick him up after school."

"Thank you, Tasha."

She takes him along to school, with her four-year-old daughter Angela, who is similar in appearance to her, before she goes to work.

"Did you watch the news, Teal?"

"No, and I wish not to hear about any news until my arrival to work so then I'll look in the paper."

"Ok then have a good day Teal."

"I'll meet you later this afternoon for lunch at the Dott. Brent, have a good day at school."

Watching Brent leave I noticed that he looks so much like his father. They both have a nice smile, bright beautiful skin and brown eyes. His father left me for a situation that happened in the past. I'll never forget what happen that day. He won't forgive me, perhaps when he does, maybe I'll stop having these dreams.

First, I will drink some coffee, then take a shower and go to work. I work as Head Coordinator of the youth center for rehabilitation of children and young adults between the age of twelve and sixteen. These kids I work with have been detained for a variety of crimes, theft, and destruction of property, failure to attend school, and unruly behavior at home and in public. We even have the ones that have taken illegal drugs. Some are on medication for their behavior. I currently have a sixteen-year-old young man who has been there since the age of thirteen.

He has committed the crime destruction of property on many homes, spraying graffiti on the houses. Finally, these properties were cleaned and repaired. The homes are back to normal, and he will join the prison society soon where he will remain for the rest of his sentence possibly for a couple more years. Finally, I'm ready for work except my gun. They took my gun away from me, but I have it back now. It's locked up in the closet in a safe place I always carry it especially when I'm working it is the last thing I get besides my purse on the way out the door.

Peace and quiet I enjoy while I'm driving to work. I've had this position for three years now. My former job was a Gang Squad police officer. A scholar of law, I served ten years on the police force after completing high school then I entered the police academy. While working as a Gang Squad Officer I studied Law at the University. Then I had a baby.

13

Graduating from Law School. Now I need to pass the Bar exam to receive my license to practice law. I have arrived at the center and only allow good morning spoken at the beginning of the day at this place.

"Good morning Teal."

"I hear the kids chant, and I reply back."

"Good morning and I hope everybody is doing a great job, so they can leave this place."

I see Thomas and greet him, "Good morning."

Thomas is the Assistant Director of the youth center. He is very understanding, a strict follower of the laws and conduct of the youth in public, and at the center. Thomas is there to enforce the proper rules for the center to remain in good standing with the state.

He said, "Did you hear the news yet?"

I replied, "Wait first before you explain let me get another cup of coffee."

As I pour the hot coffee Thomas is describing the incident.

"Well we have another one this time he is a fourteen-year-old boy that has committed the same crime destruction of property spraying graffiti on the homes. Just like the other boy has done spraying the letter Z indicating the gang from the Zoo. The detectives sent him here and want him evaluated to see if it is gang related like if it's starting again."

I responded, "Thomas there haven't been any gang related crimes since we shut that operation down six years ago. Why can't they take on this task? Talk about conflict of interest. Why can't they watch the boy or send him somewhere else?

Thomas replied, "To prison with the adults, anyway his parents are here." Did you talk to them Thomas? "Certainly, I did, they're stressed and don't have an ideal." What about the fourteen-year-old perpetrator? "He won't talk so I have no way to account what happened other than this information the detectives brought over in his file so here it is." Boldly I picked the file up and went to talk to his parents. As I approach them what a view the mother is crying, and the father has the look of having no clue about situation Thomas is right. They are stressed, their son just committed the crime destruction of property, and encouraging gang activity it will send him to prison after he reaches the age of sixteen.

"I am director Teal Tace. Do you understand the charges your son is to face the destruction of property spraying graffiti on descent homes and expected of gang association?" Crying, the mother said, "Can you please help him?" Well we can start with this first question? "What is the name of the gang?" Both parents appear with a puzzled look on their face the dad said, "He's not in a gang."

"Dad, do you understand the charges?"

He has no explanation.

Obviously, he's clueless. "They sent your son here, so he can avoid residing in jail now, with adults until he is the age of sixteen. I will see what I can do, but it doesn't give me control of keeping him here at the institution. That is for the judge to decide. I can only recommend therapy with a psychiatrist, and you need to find a defense lawyer for him. This investigation will take until the end of the day. So you can stay here at the center in the waiting room until this evening or choose to go home. Your son isn't going anywhere unless the detectives that brought him here pick him back up." I thought, I am not amused, and they don't have a lawyer. Wishing this situation wouldn't have happened again because of the new law. Therefore, I must be mentally strong to take on this task. On the other hand, eventually Thomas will work on this case. On my way to see the perpetrator reinforcing these kids has always been my way of doing things, but in this case, it's going to be a challenge. It is hard enough to make the person that has committed the crime speak. I need to know. Why he has done this?

I walk in the room and slam the door! Bold in every way, I stated, "My name is Teal Tace and we need to talk. Your life depends on it. What gang do you belong to?" He is mute, "Why did you do this?" Waiting for an answer, still waiting I said, "Cat got your tongue? One more minute, or you go directly back with the detectives that brought you here. They will have no mercy for you, and your mother is pleading for my help." Crying he said, "I didn't mean to do it." Where did you get the ideal to destroy the homes with that spray? Who told you to do this?

He explained, "I heard the story about the Zoo, and wanted to spray a home." I replied. "How dare you spray that Z, on them homes? You are lucky you didn't physically hurt anyone. One more question? What does the Z mean to you?"

He said. "The Zoo it was a mistake I was trying to be cool."

Suddenly! I'm remembering what Brittany told me that day. She said, "He's leaving the Zoo. I love him." Then I focused back to the conversation.

"I will put you in a room. You will act, speak, and do as you are told. If we hear you mention the Zoo again and that Z sign, your ass is grass. Don't get too comfortable things might change time to talk to your parents one more time, young man."

I walked out the door feeling a bit of fright thinking about the Zoo, because I remember the Zoo very well when I worked in GS, Gang Squad that was one of our projects. We were to watch a jungle of rough boys that were ignorant, selfish fools who sold drugs to kids. Like in a wilderness the neighborhood couldn't move forward because of the noise of gunfire, fatality and disputes. The neighbors were so intimidated that they moved out of their homes because of these reckless people who acted like wild animals with weapons. We worked hard on the investigation, surveillance, inspections, and expectations, of them to stop, to shut it down. I informed the parents the center would give him a room here for the day. "I will investigate the case and tell the judge about the research. He'll go to court tomorrow and I'm sure the prosecutor will want to trial him as a minor. Be here at ten o'clock sharp."

They said, "Thank you!"

I turned and left. "Thomas can you tell the men to give him a room and food?"

"Yes, no problem."

"I'm going to meet Tasha at lunch now plus I'm going to inquire more information about the case at the Dott."

Ever since I left GS my duty is to redeem these young people who commit these senseless, but very severe crimes for the society to stay secure. The streets are filled with cars and people walking on the sidewalks as I go to meet Tasha at the Dott. It is a restaurant that I've been going to for many years. A diner, also the meeting place for the officers, detectives and others from the community. Many emotions unfold at the Dott. We've had good celebrations and sad times there. I need to see what has happened. So, I can stop this cycle that resulted with me making a huge sacrifice in the past for us to keep the peace. "Good afternoon, Tasha."

"How is your day going Teal?"

"Fair except this job can be overwhelming I replied while I set the file on the table and sat down. The waitress arrived and asked, "Ready to order?" Tasha answered, "The regular for us, two orders of French fries, and two iced teas. Teal look at your man he has a new friend." Looking over at the dining bar, I see Brent's father with his new female partner, then asks Tasha.

"She looks familiar is that Julie? She was a rookie when I left. She's a detective now?" I thought she is cute, but I barely know her. She has short hair, and a beautiful innocent face but a demeanor of toughness just like Brittany had. It doesn't bother me that he has another girl; maybe just a little because he is such a handsome man and looks attractive in that shirt with his tie on I'm so proud of him. Oren is a detective now. Julie leaves and he's coming over here. He said, "Move over," then helped himself to some of my fries. I uttered, "Oren, can you get your own?" He replied, "Wait! Why do you have that file here? "Oren, I need to do some research on this young man. "Teal send him back to the prison and let the judge decide. We can't have these young people trying to start something that is over." I immediately responded.

"Wait a minute, Oren. Your people sent him to the center for us to watch!"

Oren replied, "The chief sent him! Teal stop trying to take back." Tasha said, "Hold on Oren."

BREAKING NEWS!

Everyone is looking at the television hanging on the wall. The Warden of Lastview has pasted away from natural causes surrounded by his family, details later the four o'clock news, back to regular programming. "What I was trying to say, Teal you can't bring them three back, and change young criminals like that into better people. You already have a boy there now going to prison for the same crime."

"Well Oren, with the new law applied, and him being so young in that atmosphere, I can keep him at the center, so he can forget about the Zoo. Also, it will stop him from going to that prison so soon to make up the time. I knew I wouldn't get any support here. Just don't forget to pick Brent up from school. I'm going now Tasha, I'll call you later." She said, "Teal, what about your fries?"

I replied, "No I'm full, you can have them Oren

excuse me I have to go." I stormed out of the restaurant and got into my car with feelings of disappointment. I started to sob, and thought Oren is right I cannot change this. I can't change us. Finally I'm back to the center. Thomas asked, "How was lunch? Did you gather some more information?" No Thomas, just that the Warden of Lastview has passed away. When it comes to the boy we'll let the judge decide. We will inform the judge that we have room for him here at the center until he is the age of sixteen. "Good decision, Tea." Many call me Tea for short, including Thomas. Is it alright if I leave early Thomas? "Teal is there something wrong?" No, I need to take care of some business. I go sometimes to where Brittany is laid to rest, because of the peaceful sense. I say all the time, "Brittany what shall I do? Oren despises me. He's trying to pretend that day didn't exist, but the big mistake is the turmoil." I feel like she is saying the times I visit.

"It was not your fault. Tell him what really happened that day then move on Teal." Which sets me a little closer to progress.

Chapter 2
Move On

I arrived home earlier than usual so I'll take this time to nap until Oren brings our son home. On occasion I don't get much sleep. Trying to move on studying for the law exam, and the dreams about Brittany. Except this time, the dream I had was different. I've dreamed about the Warden of Lastview prison and he spoke. "*Move on you'll do a good job.*" Suddenly I awoke. I'll do some research on the computer. Type in the Warden of Lastview only a profile, but wait the job is already available.

Qualifications are

- *Must have a Law degree or either some legal experience, and occasionally attend court.*
- *Must comply with all of the past and present laws, that have been applied.*

- *Must be willing to work with people who serve the city, the Mayor, Governor.*
- *Must have Supervisory skills and Law Enforcement experience.*
- *Only a full and thorough resume will be accepted.*
- *Send to the Attention of District Attorney Barron Adams.*

I thought should I send my resume I have some law enforcement experience, and soon I will take the test to become a licensed attorney.

So, I sent my resume.

SENDING

I can hear the doorbell.

FINISHED

It's Oren and Brently at the door I pressed the button to let them up. Brent runs in.

"How was your day at school?"

"I read to the class all by myself today."

Then he ran straight for his toys, the various superhero action figures.

24

"Very good sweetheart," I replied. Oren enters as well. He asked, "Why did you leave your lunch?"

"I was there for information, and you made it clear, that I was just wasting my time." As I walked away he grabbed my hand. Then he pulled me close to him softly whispering." I miss you Teal." What about Julie? He put his hands on my head and started to kiss me. "Wait a minute. What about Julie," I asked? "She's a friend can I stay tonight? Yes, he did just like the other times we made love. So, I'm not surprised Oren is the only man I've loved. I couldn't resist him. With the both of us moving on with our lips locked, physically his loving fits me like a glove of love, only I wish it was enough to bring back the trust, but now emotionally it would be too tough, with the situation, both of us aren't sure that we should even be together. It is ending now, and the two of us have fallen over to sleep until late after midnight Oren's phone rings while he is sound asleep I awake. "Oren your phone is ringing, answer it." Instead he rolled over and turned it off with both of us falling back to sleep meanwhile the sound of the doorbell! Someone is visiting at three in the morning, so I arose to answer it.

"Who is it," I asked?

25

"It's Julie, is Oren here?

He's supposed to come home tonight, and he better make up his mind." Hold on wait a minute. Oren, Julie is here, I thought she was a friend. Are you living with her?

"What time is it? I was going to tell you but."

"Oren it's three in the morning."

"Teal I'm sorry I have to go."

So, I sat down on the bed and took a deep breath. He left again after touching my body and heart. After that emotional situation I just needed to lay down and sleep to think it over. I wonder if I will ever love again and didn't know they were living together he will never touch me again.

Ring! The alarm clock and now it's time to get up this morning with the same routine, preparing Brently for school again. There's the doorbell! Excited, I approached the door to tell Tasha the news.

"I sent my resume out."

"Where Teal?"

"I want you to guess."

"To be a detective?"

"No, the biggest job ever, the Warden position at Lastview Prison!"

"Teal I thought you were overwhelmed with the coordinator job at the youth center."

"Yes, but this will be a better challenge."

"What about the incident with you and Brittany?"

"It's over already. It was proven, self-defense in my favor."

"Dismissed!" You're right Tea. "Anyway, Tasha that happened six years ago I'm done with school, and I have my gun back now." She gave me a hug, as I thought except dismissed in the dreams I have.

"That's a good idea Teal I'm glad you're happy."

"I sent my resume to the District Attorney Barron Adams."

"Well, congratulations and thank God it's Friday is Brently ready?"

"Yes, thank you for taking him to school. This morning I'm supposed to be in court, and I expect Thomas to prepare our case."

"Good morning Thomas. What's the status?"

He replied, "Just waiting to see if you want to intervene on this young boy's behalf. He is to be prosecuted by Adams in about an hour."

"Thomas can you take on the case this time? I would rather complete the transfer for the sixteen year old young man to go to prison." As I looked at the sixteen-year-old young man's file for the last time I write.

The young man has completed rehabilitation. He has done well with therapy, and he understands the crimes he has committed were wrong. We have kept him here, with observation. Only to wish him well in the future. The young man has done a good job, with time served of three years. Please have mercy on the decision, decided of his future stay at Lastview.

Sincerely Teal Tace

Later Thomas has returned. "Thomas I'm done with the transfer."

"How did it go in court with the new boy?"

He replied, "The judge and D.A. have agreed for us to keep him here at the center until the age of sixteen. Then complete his stay as an adult in Lastview. We are stuck watching him unbelievable; one in, and one out funny how things happened."

I said, "Thanks Thomas."

Finally, the work for the week is complete, and I meet with Tasha to play racquetball. The conversation this evening was telling her about last night, as I had the first serve.

"Oren will not touch me again! Julie showed up at my residence last night unexpectedly, looking for Oren."

Tasha said, "The nerve of her, I can't believe it!"

Then she returned the ball.

I uttered, "He lives with her and is probably telling her; he occasionally just stays there at night for our son."

"Teal, do you love him?"

I replied as I tried to catch my breath, "I'm not sure. He didn't tell me they were living together."

As I leave the gym what a day both of those kids got a break, and I'm glad it's over.

Doorbell! Oren?

"Yes Tea, it's me open the door."

Standing there holding Brent in his arms.

I said, "Oren, I asked you not to carry him.

He's getting too big for that, and you're wearing your gun."

"Teal, safety is always on."

"Right, like I was safe last night."

"I'm sorry about that. Let me explain."

"No, worry about your gun! Come on Brent, go play with your toys."

As tears filled my eyes I won't make the same mistake twice, "Thank you Oren for picking him up from school and bringing him home."

"Teal wait!"

He said, "Can I come in, so we can talk?" "No, I don't want to talk about it."

Meanwhile, Oren stood there, and I shut the door. Time to relax and have a glass of wine Brent is asleep so I sit here in the chair thinking about her again. I remember when I'd first found out about it. When I worked as a Gang Squad Officer she was my partner Brittany. She is Oren's younger sister. Brittany and Oren followed in their father's footsteps as police officers. My sister Tasha, and I were always interested in serving the public as well. On the other hand, Brittany was beautiful, with sort of a tough, stubborn mood. She wore her hair styled to the back with an innocent face, beautiful complexion, and sparkling eyes, around my height 5'5". The days I often visit in my mind that one day I will never forget out of the three years of us working at the gang squad together trying to stop that war.

After all the hard work, surveillance, investigation, many arrests, and most important risking our lives in gun battle at the Zoo. If I can only go back and change that day while we changed out of our uniforms, in the locker room.

"Glad the shift is over Brittany?"

"Yes, and I am going Teal."

"Lately you've been rushing, Brittany. Are you all right?"

"Of course I am just anxious to go home."

"Aren't we all, Brittany? Well before you leave. Did you receive the information? I tell you we are going to officially bring the other three Zoo members in for arrest."

She looked and said, "No I wasn't aware."

Then she slammed the door to her locker saying goodbye. Brittany was moving so fast she dropped her wallet on the ground I had noticed on my way out of the station. So, I decided to take it to her apartment. I arrived there taking the elevator up. When I arrive to the floor walking off to stroll down the hall, I saw her and him laughing.

She said, "I miss you Samuel."

I thought wait a minute she has a boyfriend. I didn't want to interrupt. Shocked, I slowly turned my back. Then quickly went the other way where they couldn't see me.

He said, "I miss you too."

Then she closed the door. That voice, and his face he looked familiar I can't forget a face. I remembered he is one of the three members of the Zoo, who is on the list to be picked up we interrogated him Samuel. They call him Sam.

What if Oren found out? His sister is involved with a gang member in the same way because my heart dropped! So, I waited until the next morning to confront her. At that time, I was thinking how serious I must be, when addressing her about it, before telling Oren. In tears I sit here and reminisce it was her wallet.

"Brittany, you dropped your wallet yesterday, and I attempted to take it to your apartment last night."

I will never forget the blank look on her face when she asked.

"Where is it?"

I gave it to her and uttered, "I saw the one they call Sam there with you. He's on the list to be picked up."

She said, "Keep your voice down, Teal his name is Samuel."

I warned her, "Brittany, this Samuel is a suspect, you can't trust him. We both interrogated the man when we picked him up. Oh no, did you fall for him? He is part of the Zoo, I'm telling Oren."

Brittany pleaded, "No, I love him. He's innocent and leaving the Zoo. Anyway, if you tell Oren, I declare I'll mention to him about you, and his partner Wills."

I said. "Wills? What about Wills?"

I was having a flashback then about that day with Wills.

"Keep your hands to yourself Wills, or I'm telling Oren!"

Wills replied, "I'm just joking Teal."

"Well I don't think it's funny."

I told her that nothing had happened.

"Nothing happened."

She uttered, "You told me yourself that Wills made you feel uncomfortable, be quiet, and relax. Samuel is my business. Here comes Oren now."

Then she walked away.

He spoke. "Ladies, time for roll call."

I stood there in shock and thought, she's got me I can't let Oren find out about Wills making a pass at me. We're all working great together to shut them criminals down, and I was expecting a baby during that time I didn't tell anyone about it then, not even her. Remembering that day, I sit here in the chair with tears rolling down my face. On nights like this I really remember that time very well, because I decided not to tell Oren and regret it. I should have told him the truth about Wills, Sam, and Brittany over, and again. Now I have feelings of anxiety, and guilt that things could have been different.

The weekend is over. I'm back to work at the youth center. The day started slow. I'm sitting with Thomas. I'll call Oren to confirm if he'll pick Brently up from school. Ring! "Hello this is the police department. May I help you?"

"Tasha this is Teal, is Oren in?"

"Yes, but he is talking to the District Attorney."

"Would you like to wait?"

"Yes Tasha, how is your day going?"

"Good, Teal. What about yours? Slow." I said.

"Hold on, he's available now."

"Hello, Oren, this is Teal."

"Sorry I was talking to the District Attorney he was here and will not prosecute the drug traffic suspect we've been investigating.

We had the perpetrator and now must let him go, he claims we don't have enough evidence."

"Will you pick Brent up?

I need to study."

"Only if you let me bring something to eat over and a movie."

"Fine Oren." I'm finally at home so I'll check my e-mail before I review for the exam. A message from Lastview. They have accepted my resume. Interview with District Attorney Barron Adams at one-thirty on Friday! I'm so excited. This is good news!

There is the doorbell, and they have arrived. I thought, should I tell Oren the news about the interview? No, I'll wait. He brought my favorite sandwich corned beef and a movie. I sit and watch the movie with him. He is twisting my hair. I usually style my hair pinned up, but this afternoon it's hanging down on my shoulders. Oren is rubbing my thighs, laughing as we watch the show it's very entertaining to him, but I don't feel entertained with his hands on my thighs.

"Oren stop!" I said. At this point he was drinking wine stating, "I want to be here."

"No Oren, I'm tired of being in the middle of you and Julie."

I looked at him in the eyes and stated, "You don't know what you want."

He replied, "I'll leave then."

So, he arose took the movie with nothing else to say. I sat there thinking when he stays I don't have these dreams about Brittany, because of the guilt I feel, somehow, I must move on.

Chapter 3
Lastview

Friday's the job interview for the Warden position at the prison Lastview. Tasha and I look through my closet for business attire presentable for me to wear. I know I'll style my hair pinned up.

"Tasha, I found something. What about this outfit?"

"Teal, that suit is perfect."

"Tasha, tell me about Mr. Barron Adams, I don't believe I've ever met him with only Thomas going to court for us."

She replied, "He's something of a man Teal, tough, smart, and very graceful. He is also nice, handsome, and professional he visits the station, and the crime scenes."

"Tasha, I hope I'll feel comfortable in his presence."

The end of the week has arrived. The day is Friday so I'm on my way to work at the youth center. I will work until it's time for lunch, then go back home to shower and change for the interview. The time is here, and I'm nervous as I have arrived at The Law Office of District Attorney Barron Adams, and Firm.

"Good afternoon Ms. Tace," the secretary said. "You may have a seat. Would you like coffee, tea or soda?"

I replied. "No, thank you."

Feeling sort of uneasy sitting and waiting, I thought I see there are no other females here, and imagined being the only girl, in which I should be used to it, for years I worked around mostly men, so I sat patiently and waited.

The secretary said, "Ms. Teal Tace the D.A. will see you now."

I thanked her and proceeded to the interview. When entering his office, he was sitting in a nice chair behind his neatly arranged desk. I admired his law licenses, and degrees hanging on the wall, along with a beautiful painting above a library shelf filled with case word files books, The Black's law dictionary Federal, State and compiled register law books, encyclopedias, standard dictionary's, books in alphabetic order as well. Then Mr. Barron Adams stood, and greeted me with a handshake.

Hello, be free to have a seat he said as he sat back down in his chair, I noticed that he is a very attractive man, with beautiful features. A clean cut straight black spiked head full of hair, freshly shaved face, and beautiful skin, to accompany his nice body, also his hands were soft. "Thanks for being present. I must say this resume is very impressive. Ms. Teal Tace the director of the youth center. I can't believe we have never met before."

I replied, "Thomas, the other director is usually present in court."

He speaks. "Yes, Thomas. Just the other day we settled a case in court involving a young man. Well let me explain, the position is Warden of Lastview. The Chief Administrator of the prison Ms. Tace I picked out your resume, because the job can be stressful, and intense however, looking over your work history, I see you have worked some time as a Law enforcement officer, ten years. There is a large staff at Lastview. The prison is obviously much larger than the youth center. You will oversee the staff and prisoners. Lastview carries capital punishment now so you will coordinate the death penalty. I'm looking for an individual that can be bold, professional, and have no personal feelings about the laws ever leaving any room to be gullible. A Warden who will carefully interview each inmate up for a review, and report their behavior status to me, then after that I will introduce your report to the parole board, to decide if Lastview will be their last view of the prison. Tell me about your former job as a police officer."

At this point I'm daydreaming about what happen that day, sitting on the sidewalk as I held Brittany. I thought I've seen blood, pain, and tears oblivious to the war of violence and crime.

"Ms. Tace?" I looked up.

He asked, "Are you, all right? You look as if your mind is wandering."

"Oh, I'm sorry, the job helped me pay for law school. "The position paved the way sir."

"Right here it says that you have completed law school."

"Are you a Lawyer?"

"No sir, I still need to pass the Bar examination."

"What will be your area of practice?"

"A Civil Law Lawyer."

He laughed, "A Civil Law Lawyer!"

He is so amused. His laugh was refreshing.

", I hold a Master's Degree in Federal and Criminal law but I also practice it Civil law, plus Political law. These are my favorites working for the people. Ms. Tace, now tell me about you?"

"I have a six-year-old son, and enjoy a variety of hobbies, reading, some yoga, but most of all I enjoy spending time with him."

"Ms. Tace, I have one more question? How do you feel about capital punishment?"

I responded, "It was the new law appointed, and the state carries it now at Lastview."

Mr. Barron looked at me and laughed. Then he took his glasses off, and his eyes were so attractive I knew he was beautiful and confident sitting upright in his chair, Mr. Adams asked point-blank.

"Do you carry a gun?"

I thought. How did he know that? The gun is strapped to my inner thigh.

"Yes, sir I have a license to carry the weapon."

"Teal, the duties of a Warden affect an entire community. So, you'll be assigned occasional appearances in the courtroom, meeting with people who currently serve the public, the Mayor or the Governor. Trust me, like you're working with

Thomas. There is the next man in charge Leo, and many who are third in command, a staff, but one chief the Warden of Lastview."

Finally, he stated. "The interview is complete."

I thanked him for meeting with me.

"My pleasure I will make the decision. It will be through direct call contact."

He walked me out to the secretary's desk. I told them to have a good day then left. Did you find a warden? The secretary asked.

"Yes, a woman." He said.

"Call her at the end of the day. Tell her to put in her two weeks' notice for the present job she serves. Then send her an employment package."

"Yes, sir," the secretary replied.

The message was left on the answering service when I arrived home. I was hired for the job as Warden of Lastview, and anxious to start! The first day I'm to report to the D.A.'s office for orientation. Tomorrow, I'll inform Thomas and the City. This is a powerful position, and I want this power after fighting that war in the past while working as an officer. So excited and satisfied about getting the job I retired to bed.

Dreaming, about Oren screaming.

"Teal! No Brittany!"

"What happened?"

"Why are you two doing out here?"

"Who did this?" Sirens!

I screamed she brought us here! Alarm! I awoke to shut it off, soon I'll need to tell Oren the truth about the dream, and what happened that day, because again, and again I can hear him screaming. Well the two weeks are complete. Thomas has the position of director now of the center, and he is well qualified.

Today is the big day. I start my new job. District Attorney Barron will accompany me to Lastview. The first rule was boarding a vehicle from the back of his office. I can ride the bus like everyone else who works at Lastview, or either take a car. D.A. Barron and I took a car driven by an armed guard. He opened the door and offered.

"After you, Ms. Tace,"

I replied, "Thank you, Mr. Adams."

He explained, "Teal, this laptop computer is the file it's for you and has a list of all the inmates at Lastview. This is a business phone to directly speak with me and the other staff. Recorded on the laptop is a profile of their records, crimes committed. Let me get to the point, Teal. I need someone to look over the prisoners' files to see if they are worthy of re-entering society. You will start interviewing them thoroughly. Then completing an explanation as to why they should or should not stay at Lastview. I'll review the results you recommend and, introduce them to the parole board, then we'll see if they'll take it into consideration. The easy part is the staff. You will be able to control them, but when we get there I will first introduce you to the next man in charge, Leo. He is the Assistant Warden and will be there for you, especially to deal with the most dangerous inmates who reside in the penitentiary block. Turn the music on please."

He said, "I hope you don't mind Piano Concerto #23 by Mozart the great classic."

Arriving to Lastview the first stop is the place where everybody checks in their belongings before entering the prison ground. Leo is awaiting our arrival in the prison.

"Well we are here at Lastview, a facility built about twenty years ago," said the D.A.

I believe I haven't visited Lastview before, because when I worked as an officer, we were mostly confined on the streets to fight crime. The prison seems to be as I imagined, a fresh landscape of flowers, bushes, and shrubs. I suppose the trees are about thirty-feet high surrounding Lastview, also a high fence, and a towering security area that is twenty-four-hour surveillance with armed guards. We have arrived at the security gate to check in. Mr. Adams showed his I.D. badge to them.

"Ms. Tace this is where you will get out of the car to have your belongings checked."

There stood two guards, heavily armed. "Welcome to Lastview, District Attorney Barron."

The other guard nodded his head. "Hello, this is Teal Tace the new Warden."

"Welcome, any weapons or belongings?"

The guard asked? "No, but the Warden does carry, I'll let her explain."

"I carry a 38-caliber gun, my purse, and the inmate file as well as my business phone and personal phone."

They looked in my purse as, they are cautious.

The guard stated, "You're clear now Warden. This is your I.D. badge to access all departments. Have a good day."

"Ms. Tace, I must explain. Over the last five years, besides the courtroom, Lastview has been my second home. I'll do the orientation."

"Barron! You finally made it. Sorry about the Warden, he was a good man."

"Leo, this is Teal Tace, the new Warden."

There he stood. The second man in charge Leo, a tall, dark, well-built man.

"Nice to meet you Ms. Tace," said Leo.

The D.A. said, "Leo, that's Warden Tace. We should tour now."

The inside of the prison is clean with the smell of pine, and the floors shine. Walking with the D.A. and Leo, they show me around. I see the cellblocks, and steel bars and the cellmates they guard.

On our way to the basement is where the staff headquarters, kitchen, and the commissary are, also the place where my office is located, I left the file and my purse in it after we briefly looked at it, then we proceeded to a door with a sign that reads: "I.D. badge required gaining access to the stairwell." Mr. Adams walked in front of me, as we walked up one flights of stairs. Leo followed behind me. Lastview is a coed facility. The female inmates reside on the first floor. I met the guard staff, which included mostly female guards, and four men who were their reserves for extra protection.

"Welcome, Ms. Tace," they spoke.

I replied, "You can call me Warden Tea."

The three of us walked upright past the female inmates.

"Traitors!" One of the women screamed. Then she spit in District Attorney Barron's face!

He ordered, "Leo, spit mask for that inmate. How dare she do that?"

Leo used his radio to notify someone to attend to the woman. "D.A. Adams I can't believe she did that why would she do that?" I asked. But he disappeared. Walking away only to find himself nervous, shaken up in the men's room, removing his glasses, turning the water on, and washing his face. "Damn, where's my handkerchief? Trouble-making bitch I forgot you were here." He mumbled as he dried his face and cleaned his glasses. Then he lifted his head up and looked in the mirror. Remembering when he couldn't take his eyes off her. She was once capable of turning him on he remembered, as he shut the water off mumbling, "Bitch I know how to turn you off."

"Excuse me Warden. Right this way. Sorry about that inmate some of them think we're traitors all because they want special favors. Barron will be back," said Leo. The next floor is three more fights up to separate the women from the men. "Men!" Leo shouted, "This is your new Warden, Ms. Teal Tace. Please conduct yourself appropriately as she will observe the facility."

He continued to show me around. Each floor has three sections. Section one is for First time offenders. Section two, these are Second cycle inmates on record for violent crimes. Section three, armed robbers. The men behind bars looked about except I hear, "Good morning, Teal." I've heard that voice before. It was the sixteen-year-old young man that was transferred from the center. "Good morning," boldly I replied.

Suddenly beep, beep. Leo's phone rings. He answers it. "Yes sir."

"Leo, I will be up in a minute, but between you, and me, have that bitch transferred out of Lastview immediately," ordered the D.A.

"No problem, sir. That was the D.A. he will meet us upstairs."

Leo said, "Three more fights to the last floor."

The D.A has met us at the Section for inmates awaiting capital punishment, the last level up."

I approached the floor looking around daydreaming about the rifle, and that day Wills said they're better off dead. The D.A. returned. "So, how's the tour? He startled me! "Sorry Warden Tace as you see I'm not liked by some of the inmates. This is the last floor for those that will receive the death penalty fortunately the floor is empty, and we haven't put anyone here yet." That's it now, we're finished with the tour, and it's time for us to return to the basement to meet the others," he said. "Attention staff, this is your new Warden If you have any questions or concerns, inform her right away! Standing straight and courageous, I thought of all the officers, and prisoners who might take orders from me.

Finally, we are back in my office. "I will bring lunch back as the Warden settles in, said Leo."

"So, do you like the office that will accommodate you? Yes, so sat in my chair, and looked at the file on the desk. The office is clean and empty. The former Warden is no longer here. Mr. Adams sat next to me as he talked about the information in the file. While he spoke I couldn't help but admire his tie, and the fresh smell of his bright, fragrant cologne. Then he looked at me in my eyes, and stated sincerely, "The facility is home to two hundred inmates, 100 men on one floor; 100 women on the other, and as you see no one is awaiting capital punishment." In the folder is a description and updates on each person. You need to review their behavior. Chart the progress for every inmate as honestly as possible completing at least ten by the end of the week. Do you think you have any questions?"

"Yes sir. Why did that female inmate do that?"

His response, "You don't have to worry about her one less problem for you to deal with, so we already took care of that." Leo has arrived back from the kitchen, bringing lunch for us to sample.

"Ms. Tace, I must now leave. Thank you for the lunch Leo, but I've had my welcome today. May I have a word with you? Leo, I know she's a woman like the other females on the staff protect her. Leo said, "Aye, aye, sir."

As the day moved on I had time to talk to one inmate in for drug charges he has served five years with good behavior. No problems have occurred. So

I recommended this man for probation, and a final stay at Lastview.

The day has ended, and I'm scheduled to meet Tasha at the Dott. Surprise! A surprise party to celebrate my new job as the Warden. Many were there including Wills, who crept up behind me, and picked me up. "No!" Then there is Oren who approached me and clapped.

"I can't believe you Teal, the Warden of Lastview I'm surprised. What about your pursuit to be a lawyer?"

I replied, "I can actually still do that there. I'll be in court with District Attorney Adams. Where is Brent?"

"He's with Julie, and will stay overnight I have to go," he said.

"Enjoy your night."

In the meantime, I sit and drink with feelings of disappointment here at the Dott. I cared that Oren is slipping away. He must really like Julie to ignore me, and let her watch our son, so I laughed with the others then returned home alone, undressed myself, took a shower, and went to bed.

Tomorrow is my second day at Lastview. Working this morning I started with two interviews; to conclude the two inmates proved to be worthy of release stating to Leo, "Interviewing the prisoners takes time. The D.A. has made it clear ten by the end of the week."

"Take your time I'm sure you'll do a good job."

"The District Attorney will be pleased," said Leo.

"Good morning Barron, this is the Governor."

"Good morning sir."

"How is the new Warden working out for you?"

"She has started, and I'm waiting for explanations and for her to recommend inmates who shall be released."

The Governor replied, "So you hired a woman? Don't forget about Friday evening dinner and cocktails, also expensive cigars. Invite her as well, so we can meet the new Warden of Lastview."

Immediately, the District Attorney contacted me.

"Warden Tace, the interview with the prisoner whom served five years. I agree with that review and the parole board. So, congratulations, Warden. Friday the schedule for you will change for the evening. The Governor has invited his leadership staff, consider yourself part of it now. We'll go to his mansion for cocktails and dinner to discuss business concerning the State. Will you accompany me at about 6pm?" I thought the work schedule will be flexible. Suddenly I'm feeling a sense of how important this job is. I accepted. "Yes sir."

He replied, "The event is a black-tie affair, and we'll take a car. The driver will have no problems picking you up."

"I'll be ready. Thank you, sir."

When the work day ended, I went directly to the boutique to buy something to wear. I purchase a beautiful white blouse, with a long black satin skirt with a split on the side of it to access my gun.

My gun I compromise with my fashion because I carry it daily.

Chapter 4

Pardon Me

Thursday night has arrived Oren has called. "Teal, will you need me to pick Brent up from school tomorrow?"

"No, I will take him to school and pick him up. I work outside of the Lastview Prison tomorrow. In the evening I'm meeting with state leaders."

"Pardon me that's great he'll stay with me for the weekend then I'll pick him up tomorrow evening. Good Bye."

"Teal, I love your hair pinned up. You look beautiful, like you are to attend an award show, complemented Tasha."

"Thank you, Brent are you ready? Oren should be here soon, and the D.A. shall arrive with the car."

"Damn! I just dropped my contact lens on the floor of the car, I need water and a mirror."

He picked up his phone, and called my business phone.

"Pardon me, Ms. Tace I'm here at your residence. Can I use your lavatory? "Yes, look for apartment number two. I live on the second floor. The elevator will lead you to my apartment, then ring the doorbell."

"Tasha District Attorney Barron is on his way up to use the bathroom!"

Tasha asked, "How do I look?"

Before I could speak he rang the bell. It's him, so I quickly answered the elevator door which is the entrance to my place. When he walked in, we observed him in a tuxedo, he's such a handsome man, especially with no glasses on his face.

"Good evening. Thank you, I usually don't do this, but my contact fell, and I need to fix it." I said.

"No problem Mr. Adams the bathroom is down the hall."

As he turned and walked to the lavatory, Oren has arrived. Teal, what's wrong with the elevator door? I had to take the stairs." Standing there speechless I thought Tasha and I were focused on the District Attorney and forgot to shut the door. Daddy! Here comes Brent running.

Oren said, "Are you ready to go have fun?"

Mr. Adams has finished in the bathroom on his

way to leave he mentioned, "Thank you take your time I'll be waiting in the car."

I replied, "Pardon me, D.A. Adams, this is my son Brently, and I think you know my sister Tasha. This is Detective Oren Brent's dad."

He recounted. "Yes, Tasha and Detective."

So, he is offering a handshake to Oren. Ignoring the D.A.'s offer, Oren showed himself stubborn next picking Brent up carrying him out speaking,

"Pardon me I have to go."

"D.A. Adams I'm ready to go now." So, the car was waiting for us. Excited about going, it's a formal event we are attending. The driver has opened the car door for us, to the sound of music playing. "Pardon me, ladies first," D.A. Adams offered. As I sit there listening to the music I asked, "What is this song?" He replied, "My favorite Water Music by Handel, another great classic." The break I am having. Freedom from the dreams about Brittany, and the weight of animosity Oren has for me. I feel free this evening, except Oren was so rude to Mr. Adams. "District Attorney, sorry about Brent's father's manners." He replied, "Teal I have to rise above that behavior. Anyway, we had a disagreement about a man. I've been an Attorney for ten years now and was appointed by the Governor to be Prosecuting Attorney five years ago.

My parents taught me to be a good student and retain values, which include confidence, and self-determination. I have to over-look people's opinions, actions, and emotions the new law implementing capital punishment. Prosecuting it will be hard for me. It'll be my first time, but until then, I'm content with my job. It has lead me to reach goals and want changes I thought I could never accomplish. So, I'll be positive, and remain focused on the present, living each moment as if there is no tomorrow." The District Attorney continued, "Anyway you look beautiful, and I can imagine how he feels, with another man to accompany you. Don't worry about it, I've had my share of. What do they call it? Blow-Offs! So, I can sweat the small stuff. Then he lay his head back on the seat of the car, looking out the window and uttered, "As for me tonight, I wish for a quiet evening and not to think about my position."

Finally, we have arrived at the Governor's mansion the D.A. has lifted his head. The Governor's Mansion is big and beautiful surrounded by attractive scented flowers roses, tulips, carnations, and orchids. The driver has parked the car and opened the door. "Thank you," said the D.A.

For the first time in a while, I feel wonderful. I'm in a similar world, surrounded by different people. The Governor greets us. "Welcome." Governor, this is the new Warden Teal Tace." Introduced the D.A. "Thank you for joining us. Sit, eat, and enjoy," he said.

D.A. Barron introduced me to his mother, the governor's wife, and their daughter, a young lady. I also met city leaders, the mayor, and the parole board. We all sat at the table enjoying dinner served to us. D.A. Barron's mom speaks about how proud she was of her only son and, if his father was here. She professed, "God Bless his heart. I know he's proud looking down from Heaven. Our son maybe a future Governor." The campaign pictures of Barron are great as well. "Mother-no business!" The D.A. exclaimed. Then the Governor's wife stated, "Congratulations on the new job as Warden," as her daughter looked on with a smile. I replied, "Thank you, ladies."

The Governor stood up and backed away from the table. He said, "Pardon me, ladies and gentlemen.

May I borrow Mr. Adams? D.A. Barron excused himself, "I will return, everyone." I sat there enjoying the moment, listening to the classical music song, Badinerie composed by Bach.

Having dinner with the fresh scent of flowers, there is the aroma of roses in the air.

I reminisce about the last time I encountered roses.

It was at Brittany's funeral. I asked the Governor's wife, "Where are the flowers? I smell roses." She answered, "They surround the house also, and I keep a greenhouse full of flowers. Do you want to see them? So, the Governor's wife brought me to the room of flowers. Entering the place, she pointed to each one at a time. "These are my roses, carnations, tulips, and orchids."

"Light it up Barron Adams, our future Governor and here is a drink of scotch, and a cigar." declared the Governor. "The cigars are straight from overseas only the best." Cigar smoke filled the room! "How did you manage to find such a beautiful Warden? I hope she's tough," said the Governor. With the D.A looking out the slightly opened window laughing, puffing on the cigar he explained, "Tough she is as well as an ex- cop soon to be a Civil Attorney."

"Civil, the governor asked, well is she married?"

"No, but she has a son, and he has a father, that blew me off earlier. He's a detective." The Governor replied "A baby's father. Well the chances become better with a wife, Barron. Anyway, when are you going to let go, and look for love? Life is not just about a career. It's about having fun, and a family. I myself, can't wait to move my family to the Island. Your opponent has a wife and kid. It might be an advantage. Remember the race." The D.A. exclaimed, "Well, then I am sure my opponent is better than me, he is the competitor. A family man, he has his own life, and campaign, and it isn't any of my business. Besides I'm not a home wrecker."

"No. A homemaker," said the Governor while they both laughed.

"Mom, you have another guest", said the Governors daughter. "Pardon me Warden enjoy the flowers," she said. As I stood there, thinking about the scent and how much it reminds me of the flowers at Brittany's funeral, next someone asked, "Enjoying the flowers? I turned around, it was D.A. Barron. Meanwhile, I thought soon I'll need to tell him about Brittany. "Yes, I love the flowers." After conversations, laughs by all present, dinner ends with goodbyes, and nice to meet you from the guests and myself.

While we were riding home we sat quietly, and continued listening to the great classic, Water Music by Handel. He hummed. "La, la, la, la! Oh, oh, oh, oh! A great evening for a wonderful song. All, la, la, la! Lull!" Then he became silent taking a deep breath. Looking at D.A. Barron I could sense he has so much on his mind. So, I broke the silence speaking. "Thank you for introducing me to the Governor, his family, and your mom."

He responded with a smile. "Of course. My pleasure." Finally, we arrived back to my place.

He got out the car and opened the door for me. I said, "Thank you again." He said. " You're welcome. What will you do the rest of the evening?"

I thought nothing, but mentioned "Probably study for the Bar exam so I can elevate my score. What about you sir?"

"No work, a quiet evening with a good book. Usually I'm preparing for a case, but fortunately I presently don't have one. Tomorrow I'll attend to my golf game Ms. Tace. Can I ask you a question? "Yes sir." I replied. "How's the relationship between you, and your son's father why did they leave? "They are at his place for the weekend."

He reached to touch my hand, holding it he blinked his eyes. "That means he's not there. Have a good weekend."

When I entered my home with this feeling I haven't felt in a while it was his touch, also I'm amazed of the gentleman I perceive him to be. So, I took my dress off thinking, the fact is that I'm alone again.

Jingle, Jingle! That is my business phone. "Hello, Ms. Tace this is D.A Barron. How would you like to accompany me to a game of golf tomorrow morning to check out my Tee shot? Butterflies filled my stomach, I took a deep breath. "Of course, I will." Cheerfully we continued to chat the rest of the time on the phone. We're chatting about the Exam.

"What is your favorite part of the exam, Teal?"

"Law Practice Management, because maybe one day, I will organize a small firm, or either work for one."

Then we discussed the game of golf. I've never been to a golf game or played the sport. "What is the object of golf, D.A. Adams?"

"The object of golf is the fewest numbers of

strokes to advance the golf ball, so it will go in the cup, swing execute, and let it fly while enjoying the game. Usually I play the full eighteen holes, but it shouldn't take that long, because I have been working on my posture."

Under the blue skies I met him in the morning my first time attending the golf course I chose to sit on the grass; watching him on the turf I smiled, as he laughed while attending to his game. Finally, that afternoon has arrived. We departed to watch a film. While we were watching the show, he chuckled! The District Attorney is so amused. In the same way I'm also delighted.

Since the interview I feel a free spirit for myself the music he listens to, and his focus. I'm becoming aware that in the future I must forget about what I have lost in the past.

*Like An Eagle That Fly High Above Looking
Over A View Alone And Free.*

I am here on land helping him involved through the course of this most emotional, but very professional occupation.

The film has ended. He walked me to my car we said our goodnights and agreed to stay in touch. Monday has arrived, I'm back to work. Today I interviewed five inmates and recommended two that should be taken under consideration to go home. That afternoon after lunch I faxed both reviews to the D.A. He called me back immediately. "Teal, this is Barron. I agree with the interviews, signed and complete. Good job." Thank you, D.A. Barron." "Tomorrow is the big day Warden you and Leo are scheduled to be in court. I need you there to learn the routine of taking the inmate to prison after the verdict and signing the document as the Warden. May I say off the record, between you and me our recreation has really opened my eyes up to more than just work, and an occasional golf game. I want to attend the amusement park. Would you like to go this weekend? I replied, "Well I'll be spending my time with me son, but he can come with us." Great idea Teal, I will see you in court tomorrow morning."

Finally, the workday is over. I sit here happy at home. The District Attorney and I are really becoming close friends. I think we have something in common, which is making important decisions about others, an also our lives. Pleased I fell asleep, and the next morning awoke to the alarm clock only to realize I didn't dream about Brittany I'm changing because of my position.

Brent is off to school. I'm scheduled for my first day in the courtroom to see District Attorney Adams prosecuting a man for attempted murder with a deadly weapon. Apparently, the defendant had beaten the victim with a crowbar and broken his arms, legs, and ribs. The victim is in the hospital recovering, paralyzed and will need extensive therapy. "The state is calling for attempted murder," said D.A. Barron. "I'll return with the verdict," stated the judge as he slammed his gavel on the bench. The Bailiff said, "Half an hour recess." The people in the courtroom scattered, including the D.A. who walked over to talk too Leo and me. "Waiting for that verdict to see if the defendant will go back with you all to Lastview," he said. "What do you think about the courtroom Teal?" I replied, "It's what I expected." Recess is over. The honorable judge has returned.

The verdict is announced guilty with life in prison! The trial is over, and the victim's family are satisfied with the verdict. I stare at D.A. Barron he's receiving thank you, and hugs from the family members of the victim. Inspired deeply I thought, he is so tender hearted, and sincere. Most of all, intelligent. It was my first time as the Warden to sign the orders to transport the prisoner traveling back to Lastview to be locked up. Finally, I signed the paper and I, Leo, and the other officers took the man out heavily armed. They traveled with him in the police van, and I drove my own vehicle.

Back at the prison now, the inmates have planted flowers on the outside of the prison. As I walk in through the facility, I notice the floors shining, and it is lunchtime. I see the inmates doing a great job cleaning and cooking, because I can smell green peppers, onions and garlic. So, they must be preparing spicy chili, or either spaghetti, also it's a pine scent as I move along to my office. The phone in the office is ringing. The D.A. is checking again, about how I felt my first day in the courtroom? Then he expressed how excited he was to go to the amusement park this weekend. I replied, "As for the courtroom. My first day there was a touching experience, to see the family members' reaction to the verdict. I am very excited about the park this weekend too."

Chapter 5
Make You Love Me

As he jumped up and down Brent said, "Mommy, I want to ride that! "Brent hold on that ride requires waiting in line ready, it's your turn now, good job waiting, go ahead have fun." Brent is riding and waving, "Hi mommy and Mr. B." Who is Mr. B? "Well that's me, Mr. B. I told him he could call me that answered the D.A." We are having a wonderful time, but I'm exhausted, and ready to retire, with playing the game against the D.A. Shooting the water in the hole cheerfully I won the game, and I am enjoying the amusement park with my son Brent, however D.A. Barron, I observed him as having fun like a child's first trip to the amusement park.

He walked me and Brent back to our room I was tired as well as Brent, so he lay down on the bed and went to sleep. "Teal, I've had the most amazing day thank you." he replied. "Barron with all due respect to you it seems like you're missing something."

"Maybe I am, someone like you in my life," he

uttered, as he swiftly landed a kiss on my forehead. "You should talk to the detective to find out where he stands. I will retire to my room now. Goodnight and sleep well." I thought can I love again because I'm empty as I stood there. That night I slept peacefully. No dreams. The next morning, I awoke to a bright and new day full of excitement, because I love the D.A.

Oren will be here shortly to drop Brent off. I took a hot bath, washed my hair, put my robe on and, now I'm ready to rest. Doorbell!

"Thank you," I said as he carried Brent to his room. What did you do this weekend? "We went to the amusement park." He said, "With Mr. Adams!"

"Yes, Oren. Now I'm going to finish getting ready for bed."

"Teal, I really mean are you fucking him?"

"Watch your language Oren. We're just friends."

"Good," he said. "Can I fix me a drink? Oren, I'm tired."

He went in the cabinet straight for the liquor bottle, and I sense hostility as Oren took a deep breath and a couple of shots stating, "He just thinks he can compromise you, and my son especially because we were never married!"

"What are you talking about, Oren? He replied, "I know one thing he can't change." Quickly, he grabbed me! Took the towel off my head and started to kiss me. I screamed, "Stop, you're drunk and don't want to kiss me. Admit it, you just don't love me anymore! Just accept this, I have been anxious to tell you it for a while, as I didn't think or have the dream about Brittany, when you are here. She was in love with that gangster Samuel found dead in the building and I knew. That's why she took us there."

Shocked, shaking his head enraged. Oren replied, "What did you say?" She was going out with that gangbanger! Out of all honesty I told her Wills made me feel uncomfortable. She knew that he flirted with me and wanted to blackmail me by telling you. So, I kept it to myself at the time, I didn't want to cause a problem with you, and Wills but I swear nothing ever happened between me, and him." He said. "But you knew it will ruin our investigation and my sister. How could you be so stupid? It's your fault she's gone. You make me sick Teal leave me alone!" Then before he attempted to leave and get on the elevator, I was screaming, "Oren she took us there, not me! Go ahead leave again." Then I pushed him. "Now you keep your hands off me Teal, and don't you ever come near me you're a liar!" He shouted also pushing me back, I fell on the floor and begin crying out.

"That's why I have these dreams! I can't forgive myself for not telling you about Brittany! I know you don't have love for me anymore, and I can't make you love me now."

"Or make me forgive you either, damn you Teal." He said, then he walked out the door and went straight to where he could only talk and trust a couple of coworkers unable to stop his tears telling them the news as he sat in the diner they consoled him at the Dott.

That night I suffered great anxiety, remembering Wills say they're better off dead, with distress, tossing, and turning while I tried to sleep. That dream I always have. Oren screaming, "Teal!" What happened to her? No! I quietly moaned. Only to find myself awake, sitting in the corner, on the floor unable to stop sobbing in the darkness with the gun in my hand lifting the heavy black object. I felt that I despise guns, and wish they never existed, but are used for protection.

Suddenly the alarm clock rings! I hear Brent, "Mommy, it's time for school." Quietly I sat slowly to rise, next there's the sound of the doorbell It is Tasha, "Brent where is your mom? Teal, Teal!" Quickly I arose off the floor and put the gun under the pillow before she came into the room. "Did you oversleep? I was still sobbing. "It's over with me and Oren. I finally told him. He really resents me. He screamed at me, and said I took us there, and blames me for Brittany's death. Then in a rage he pushed me. Only if he just loved me like before. You know he's right Tasha It is my fault. I knew Brittany loved Samuel I should've went straight to Oren with the truth instead I messed everything up and lied. Tasha replied, "No Teal, she made that choice, you look a mess. Pull yourself together. I haven't seen you happier with this new job and don't forget about Brent." Calming down I uttered, "You're right. I must pull myself together, but I can't go to work despite the dreams. Last night was the worst night. I didn't sleep."

"I can see you've been crying all night judging from your eyes. I'll dress Brent, and you get some rest. Request the day off?"

"Ok maybe you're right I'll call the D.A.'s office to inform them I won't be in." The secretary answered.

"Law Offices, may I help you?" Slowly I said, "This is Warden Teal Tace I will not be in today I'm not feeling well." She responded, "Thanks for calling I'll tell Leo, as well as the D.A. Hope you feel better." Then I hung up and finally went to sleep.

Jingle, Jingle, Jingle, I awake and answered the business phone. "Hello, Teal. This is D.A. Barron. How are you feeling? "Not well thinking I am coming down with something."

"Well can I come to visit? No court, and I'm done here at the office, "Do you have company? "No, but." I insist, and I'll bring goodies." Then he hung up.

D.A. Barron is on his way over. I must rush, take a shower and finish my hair, looking in the mirror, my eyes are swollen from crying all night with no sleep. He'll know something's wrong, so I'll wear sunglasses. On his ride over, he's listening to Ronda Alla Turca by Mozart. Singing, "La La La. Love me! Love me, love me, and love me. Love Me! Ronda Alla Turca, All, lala! All, lala! All!" Approaching the flower shop he hums and thinks. Um! What can I take her? Some roses, then he took a trip to the store to purchase whiskey, and hot herbal tea. The perfect drink for symptoms of an illness next he returned to his car and cheerfully continued listening to the music, arriving later.

Ring! The doorbell, it's him maybe he won't stay long if I look a mess with this towel wrapped around my head and these sunglasses on. I can't let him see my eyes if he asks about them? The answer will be I have chronic allergies or pinkeye, which is the perfect idea because it is contagious I hope he'll leave. Opening the door, I turn around when he walked in. With my back turned to him I explained, "D.A. Barron you shouldn't be here I'm sick with pinkeye, and don't want you to catch it." He said, "I don't care I miss you." I asked, "How can that be? We spent the weekend together." It wasn't enough for me, so these roses are for you, and I have some fresh hot herbal tea also some whiskey."

"Thanks just leave it on the table."

"What's wrong Teal? Why do you have them sunglasses on, and why is your back turned? Why don't you look at me? "I can't do this anymore. Maybe I'm not ready." I took the sunglasses off revealing my eyes then started to cry. "What's wrong? "It's over with me and Oren. We got into a fight." He responded, "How dare Him? "No! No! It's my fault."

The volume of my voice shocked the D.A. "Teal, I see you've been hurt like other women who have come to me for help, because of these insecure men pushing them around."

"That's what he did to me; he pushed me." I described.

"I'll report him; no man has a reason to push a woman."

"You're sympathetic District Attorney. Well can you sympathize with this?"

"I divulge you D.A. Barron you'll really need this drink while I explain." First picking up the tea, and pouring him a cup of it, with a shot of whiskey in it, also filling my cup up with the two drinks as well.

"So, you haven't heard, for the last six years I've barely slept almost every night. That dream I always have about Oren's sister, Brent's Aunt Brittany she was my beautiful tough friend, and partner at GS.

On that day we were riding around patrolling the neighborhood.

Suddenly she received a call. It was Samuel he said, he was there, and finally going to tell them that he wanted out. At the end of the conversation she said, "Good luck Samuel." In the building by the

75

Zoo, the first man said, "Samuel, so you stand there a coward son of a bitch. How dare you want to leave us? We're family to the end!"

The second man spoke. "That's right your family and we don't want to disown you, over my dead body are you leaving us!" Then he lifted his gun and shot Samuel in the head. "I have to turn around!" She exclaimed. "Brittany what's wrong?" She described that, she just felt that something wasn't going right. So, she did a U-turn! Where are you going? Down by the Zoo turn the emergency lights on to the car, she said. "Brittany! Please stop! You're going too fast. So, I picked up the radio to call for help, "This is GS officer Teal! We need immediate back-up now. We are at a location near the Zoo where the gang hangs out."

Next, she stopped the car, and got out of it. She is running, I screamed. "Brittany no! Damn stop!" So, I dropped the radio, got out of the car then grabbed the gun in the back. Shaking and frightened, I ran after her. Brittany asked, "Where's Samuel?" The first man said, "Bitch get out of here! She replied, "You fucking animals killed him." When I arrived at the door, I heard a shot. Next one of them said, "Man let's get out of here!" So quietly I took the safety off the weapon. Then quickly moved behind the door so they couldn't see me as they hurried out I watched them leave it was two of them. Then Brittany wandered out. She was shot then fell to the ground. It was the last man who walked out that did it. He turned around, saw me, then lifted his gun, so insane with the gun in my hand, I shot both! One in the back, the other in his leg, lastly multiple shots to their bodies I was insane watching them fall into the street. Vengeance for her, myself, and my unborn baby. The next thing I was holding her in my arms. My pretty tough friend. Thinking all that time it could have been stopped if I would have told Oren his sister was in love.

She had fallen for the one of the members of the gang, Samuel from the Zoo. I've not told anyone except Tasha. Later the shooting was ruled out as self-defense. I was cleared. One of the saddest times at the Dott. No one ever spoke a word about it again. As for me, I only feel cold hearted. I'm unable to move on and forget that war. "What do you think about me now District Attorney, still want me as the Warden?" He replied, "Just forget about it, I love you." Then he started to kiss me. I cried. "I'm not worth it." As he was gently stroking me with his tongue, I remained quiet. Slowly we started to make love, however I felt deep down. He hadn't had a woman, because he's so aggressive in the bed. Enjoying himself for the first time like at the park and the movies, or when he is playing golf. With both of us exhausted that afternoon we drank all the whiskey and fell asleep well into the late afternoon.

The D.A awoke to his business phone jingling lying next to me he answered. Hello? "Hello, D.A. Barron, this is the Deputy Attorney. This is an emergency. Unfortunately, I have a double homicide of two young beautiful women. Would you like me to take pictures, and notes for the prosecution? They have the man in custody." "Good, send me the location on my phone, and I'll be there shortly look for me soon. A shortcut for my work, Teal my position calls I have to go sleeping beauty," he said with a kiss on my forehead. The location has been sent to his phone. He paused, as he was disturbed, and paranoid remembering, I've been to this place before. It's out there. So, he quickly entered his car. Then tuned into the great classic song, "The Sleeping Beauty Panorama," by Tchaikovsky.

Chapter 6
United

"D.A. Barron, I can't believe what happened out here. They worked right there at that Strip Club and there he is sitting in the squad car." Do you have the pictures? "Yes, I do of the crime scene and the women as well." The D.A. looked at the pictures of the two women, and uttered, "They are beautiful," as he took his laptop out to record notes. What happened? "Well apparently, he was high on drugs and attacked the lady, then her friend, next he fatally shot both. They're thought to be strippers prostituting. There they are, laying over there. The coroner has not arrived yet, but I have the pictures, and you bet he'll qualify for capital punishment. I suggest if you are elected Governor, you should shut that place down." The D.A. gasped, "No." The deputy asked, "What did you say Barron? "I know I saw them? I said, "They were beautiful."

Lost in the moment, the D.A. started to wonder

about what Teal revealed to him. The situation with her partner Brittany, never spoken again. He had been there before, also once warning a woman that if she went back here again, he couldn't help her Rema Jean. She should be thankful she's not one of them women laying in the street. Suddenly he can see Detective Oren and the Chief. So, he walked over to address them. "Detective Oren! What do we have here? Oren replied. "A double homicide." Next, he addressed the Chief. "Chief, did you know that your detective pushes women around?" The Chief said, "Who? What's he talking about Oren?" Before Oren could speak, the D.A. answered, "Warden Teal." The Chief responded. "Wait a minute. I thought you and Teal were getting along. Has there been a complaint filed?" Oren looked on and spoke. "She's the one pushing me around." Then he left. "Chief, he has anger management problems. Talk to him about it and give him some time off I think he might need it."

Later that week, Brent and I were invited to the D.A.'s house for dinner. "Welcome to my home, Teal and Brent. This is Lisa." He introduced us her. "Yes, nice to meet you Ms. Tace I've heard so much about you." I replied, "Nice to meet you Lisa. Thank you for inviting us Barron, your home is beautiful." I'll show you around, he offered.

"I'll watch Brent and finish dinner, said Lisa." Come on Brent there are lots of things for kids to do around here since Barron is a big kid, video games and, cartoons are his favorites."

"She's nice Barron you didn't mention her before."

"Lisa is my best friend, aside from her working here." So, he showed me around. "This house is lovely. I love your swimming pool surrounded by a bar to serve drinks, and a piano to play music."

He said, "Thank you. It'll be better if I can spend more time here." Walking up behind me he put his hands-on top of my shoulders. "How are you feeling?"

"Oh, my goodness, you caught me off guard. I wonder how you really feel about me revealing what happened in the past. The shooting at the Zoo, my life, and the dreams." He said, "It's in the past right? Forget about it, Lastview you work there now. Let's move on. You're safe here, this evening with dinner and music, also my mom is joining us." We did just that with his mom, dinner and music. United it was a wonderful evening.

The next month consisted of meetings with the

inmates. Many released for good behavior and time served. In the position of Warden at Lastview, I stay very busy at work. I didn't have much time for recreation. Brent went to school, and when he wasn't there he spent time with his dad, Oren, is picking him up also dropping him off. He and I only share small talk since the argument and his time off. I feel uncomfortable visiting the Dott. He and my former GS partners resent me because of my new position, and I'm sure they know the truth about Brittany, but I must not dwell on that. I have a new staff family at Lastview, and we get along great maintaining the place.

The D.A. is finishing his case. The last time I heard from him, he explained that he has been working consistently in the court, prosecuting the defendant, and has a couple of more days to go before the verdict is to be reached. He also mentioned that the hardest part for him now is proving that the women didn't harass the man for money, sex or drugs to the jury. The defendant was harassing them to sell their bodies for prostitution. Business phone, Jingle, Jingle. "Hello Teal, this is Barron."

"Hi Mr. B, I was just thinking about you. How is your case going?"

"I'm just about done. The defendant has a rap sheet in another state, and when I interviewed the eye witnesses they have no information about the young women harassing him. Just doing their job dancing at the strip club. He has no evidence, or either a character witnesses in his defense. Working on this case I've sacrificed lots of sleep, and my appetite."

"Why don't you let me bring you lunch? What would you like?"

"Whatever you see fit to bring," he replied. "Thank You."

I owe him. So, I hurried to the deli to purchase minestrone soup, salad and a deluxe sandwich topped with a variety of lunchmeat, smoked turkey breast, smoked ham, Swiss cheese and on the bottom tomatoes and crispy iceberg lettuce, on whole wheat bread. The drink will be sparkling soda water.

The secretary greets me, "Good afternoon Warden Teal."

"Hello how is your day going?" I asked.

"Great thanks for asking, and the D.A. is expecting you, so go right in."

The Music of Mozart Piano Concerto #23 was softly playing again. I'm reminded by the sweet sound of that song playing in the car riding to Lastview prison, the first day starting the position, and how nervous I was, but at the same time excited. There he is sitting in his chair. He stood up then pulled me close to him, as we passionately kissed. What about lunch? "Lunch can wait. I want to show you something." He grabbed my hand, and opened the door behind him, which leads to a room set up like a lounging area. Another office equipped with a television, black soft leather chairs, and a lavatory. Plus, electronic equipment, softly playing the music and a computer, also a phone he used to inform the secretary that he didn't want to be disturbed, as the two of us finished the case. Then he hung up. "Teal, united again. I'm so glad you're here because I miss you." I smiled and spoke. "I remember this song that first day going to Lastview. What would you have me do? He replied, "Unify." Next our lips are glued as he removed my blouse, slowly removing his pants and shirt. Now sitting on the chair, both of us are undressed. He was assertive to make love again. So, he pulled me close to open my legs, to sit on top of him, as I moved up and down. He enjoyed my breasts. Like the music playing, we made love ending with a kiss, and harmony from the song. I finally arose off him. He sat back and took a deep breath. "May I use your lavatory? He replied. "Yes." I washed my hands, next put my blouse on while I looked in the mirror as I could hear him, he was humming to the music. I thought, he's satisfied, me as well, and I am finished in the bathroom to see him on the computer.

Laying my hands on his shoulders I speak, "What about lunch? Sitting there with just his shirt and socks on he reads. "The State is calling for Capital punishment, and immediately moved to Lastview until the execution. The time has come. Now I'm finished." With a tearful expression in his eyes he looked at me, put his head up, took a breath then held it down, removed his glasses, and the tears slowly rolled down his face. I could only comfort him, with my hand on his back, as he laid his head back against my stomach. So emotional D.A. Barron's tears evaporated into my blouse then he stopped sobbing, and they began to dry, finally with a dried face he begins to eat his lunch.

"Guilty!" The bailiff read. Each person in the courtroom remained quiet. The judge declared, the decision had been made, and the defendant will reside at Lastview until the time of execution, and the staff officers will transport him back there accompanied by the Warden Teal Tace."

The defendant said loudly with hostility, "I'm not going anywhere with that bitch! All you women are the fucking same. You want a man to take care of you but think you can talk to him anyway you want to! Quickly he was handcuffed and led out the courtroom by Leo the officers as well as me, while all that were in the courtroom looked on in shock.

Suddenly my neck, the gripping pain I felt something around it pulling me back! Quickly the defendant has managed to put me in a chokehold with the handcuffs on him. The people in the courtroom screamed. "No! No!" The D.A. shouted. "Let the Warden go, she's just doing her job. Leo demanded, "Release her or we'll shoot!" With bravery I was able to reach for my weapon attached to my thigh under my skirt and, withstand the man fast, as I raised the gun, and fired a fast-single sharp shot, shooting him in the neck, resulting with him falling back, carrying me down to the floor with him, while the handcuffs remained around my neck I couldn't breathe. They were able to remove the handcuffs, transporting me to the hospital where I was slipping away. I passed out and saw Brittany and the Warden in my sleep.

She said, "I'm happy hear with Samuel, Teal don't stop being happy," and then a man appeared as well, it was the former Warden. He said, "Go back there's a job to be done as the Warden of Lastview you took my place."

Mama! Teal hang in there, we're here at the hospital. It was Brent, Tasha, and Oren. I heard them and awoke. "She's awake! Thank God," Tasha exclaimed. The doctor immediately entered the room to examine me. "Your neck looks fine, and your heart rate is back to normal. You have been in shock, experiencing injury to the most sensitive part of your neck, also a major concussion. While we repaired it, you've been in an induced coma for a week until today." The doctor said, "You'll need to heal then rest."

Tasha cried, "Teal, thank God you are all right. Don't worry about Brent. Oren will look after him. We'll leave now so you can rest." Watching Tasha leave, Oren picked up Brent, and they left. The D.A. has arrived at the hospital with orchids, only to see them leave from the room. With their backs turned while Oren carried him, Brent saw the D.A. so he smiled, and waved. The D.A. lifted his hand to wave as well also returning the smile. Finally arriving to the room, with me asleep. He placed the flowers on the table then walked over to look out the window. Exhausted I opened my eyes, speaking. "Thank you." Teal, you're awake! "Yes, just tired." He sat on the bed and wept. "I'm sorry this happened to you."

What about the prisoner? I asked? Suddenly he stopped crying, replying, "Don't worry about that get some rest I've been worried sick about you, he's not worth worrying about." What about the prisoner? The D.A. revealed he didn't make it.

"No! No! No! I started to cry. The D.A. looked on with disappointment, and boldly said, "Don't do that Teal, he was a dead man walking. What's wrong with you? We have to be strong and move on." Suddenly I stopped sobbing and didn't utter another word. He set next to me as I continued to remain quiet. Then I've fallen back to sleep. The D.A. finally has arisen. He thought she needs to rest I'll come back tomorrow. Walking to his car he could only imagine that the prisoner doesn't need capital punishment now. He sat down and started the car to quietly listen into the great classic. The Sleeping Beauty Panorama by Tchaikovsky. With tears in his eyes he's remembering Teal, Brittany, and the strippers, the convict killed, also the woman Rema Jean. He warned her years ago not to go back there. She went anyway, and she's still in jail now as a former stripper who turned to prostitution. It could have been Rema Jean laying out there, she was never the person I thought her to be except another pretty face.

The dream I had. Brittany stop! I'm holding her close to me. Brittany responded in the dream, *"Teal move on."* So I awake after a couple of weeks in the hospital. The doctor and nurse entered the room. "You're doing fine, and ready to be discharged," he said. "You have a guest too." The nurse added. "We'll get those papers ready." The D.A. has visited with a kiss on my forehead. He exclaimed, "It's been three years, and I haven't had a vacation from work. Only dedication to this job. Do you think someone can take care of Brent, and we take a vacation? Of course after you settle at home, and take care of yourself." I replied, "Yes Barron.

Where will we go?"

Chapter 7
No Not Again

Outside of San Diego, California. Upon arrival to the airport that is one of the busiest in the world. We took advantage of the car service, taking us to board a ferry to the hot, sunny, sandy beaches of San Diego, residing in a Five Star Hotel, near a place called the Rock. The great spot to stroll across the land, with a beautiful sight of the sun toned sky in the daytime, as we strolled the sandy walk on our way to the Rock, it's a place for shopping, dancing, restaurants, and a boutique. We treasured eating and drinking. Later that evening we enjoyed a charming view standing on a black rock, as we saw a big eagle flying high above free, and alone over the radiant big body of water, reflecting the sun on the big sandy beach, we remained until dusk.

Upon returning to our room overlooking the town, on a terrace. "You love to do that I said." Because he walked up behind me, and put his arms around me uttering, "I want to do it here Teal, officially marry you. It's time we move on together. Let's do this." I accepted. "I'll marry you." Tomorrow we will get a license, then go to the chapel, and elope.

That night I lay there and thought, I'm happy with Barron next to me. I depend on him, and really want to marry him except I'm so sensitive and a little determined, because when he offered to take my hand I didn't wonder like at the job interview. I said. "I will."

That morning the weather was perfect not too excessively hot. The first thing is to get ready of course I'm nervous. So, I went to a boutique at the rock. There I had my make-up done, hair styled, and bought a beautiful dress, and a golden men's ring. I'm ready to meet the D.A. at the chapel. Walking in, I met him at the altar and took his hand. We exchanged rings and vows. He smiled and said, "I will." Just as I returned the smile and said, "I will." Next, we enjoyed dinner, music, and dancing, then finished the night with dynamic love making, resulting in both of us lying in the bed exhausted, before falling asleep. We enjoyed a great vacation in San Diego.

Finally arriving home to start our new life

together we moved in with him. "Teal, I can't believe you want to bring these things. I understand your clothes and Brent's stuff, but those lamps and tables. We have everything there. You're welcome to my house now, consider it yours."

"Mine, I'll remember that, so I will make all the rules."

Laughing he said. "It's our house now."

"Thank you, Barron. I feel wonderful moving in with you, and finally I'm going back to work." "Again, you're welcome. I just want you to take care of yourself Teal, and with what happened at the court. Slow yourself down."

"I know Barron but. "Teal wait! Think about it. I'll be running for Governor, Mrs. Adams." On the other hand, the D.A. considered later she'd be a Governor's wife and the mother of his children after that, Leo as the warden.

Finally, I'm back to work at Lastview resuming reviews of the inmates. Today I reviewed three female prisoners, two of them I recommend released, but the third female inmate, Windy Rowe I was sort of concerned, because she told me they moved her cellmate. She described her as a woman behind bars for prostitution, an innocent stripper, who is spending more time in prison instead of being released, but it hadn't been addressed yet. She insisted the D.A. was holding the woman there at the prison and ordered her transferred after she spit on him. Rema Jean was her name. I remembered the situation, because I asked him why she did that? She pleaded, "Please find her, and see that she's given a fair chance." I can't promise you, but I'll see what I can do. Research showed that the first time she was released, prostitution was the charge. Then the second time around a two-year sentence for the same offense, two more years added on, next transferred the very day I started the position as the Warden of Lastview with District Attorney Barron Adams' signature. She's telling the truth. Devastated I took a quick trip to the lavatory because the news made me sick, next I consulted Leo. "This woman, Rema Jean. Why was she here for so long? Two years then transferred to another facility with more time added on four years all together?" He replied, "It was the time appointed." For prostitution? "Leo, I believe that is not correct. I will consult with the D.A. because he signed it." He responded, "With all due respect to you, Warden T.

Watch your step, she no longer resides here at Lastview. Think before you cross the line of the laws applied." Of course, all three women were put in for recommendation. The day at Lastview was not the best, learning about Rema Jean from Windy Rowe. Upon arrival to home he is not here. I'll speak to Barron when he arrives home. Sitting there waiting for him while Brent, is watching television. He is late, and I am impatient and in need of an explanation. "I'm Home Teal! Hello Brent.

What are you watching? Cartoons again, great I'll be back after I take a shower and get ready for dinner." I followed him upstairs, anxious to know. While he was taking off his suit jacket, then tie he asked, "How was your day?"

"I need to talk to you. I know we are at home, but it's about the job. Barron, I had three interviews today."

"Great I see you're getting back into the swing of things."

"Yes, but I'm concerned about an inmate - Windy Rowe's ex-cellmate." She said this woman Rema Jean was supposed to be released, but was held in prison too long." She was moved? Lisa knocks, and has a request. "How would you two like your steaks medium or well done?" We both stated, "Well." She said, "twenty minutes."

"Thank you, Lisa." Replied the D.A.

"Teal sounds to me like hearsay."

"Well I was wondering she's."

"Wait a minute!" With a temper he interrupted me. "I ordered you to not worry about her." Then he looked and declared, "Don't try to change the laws that have been applied, and I won't have you listening to gossip. Leave it alone!" So, he entered the bathroom, slammed the door, then he turned on Water Music by Handel to listen too while he showered. I couldn't believe the man who was gentle had become so harsh. I was confused. Thinking he is serious, but I was still curious. "Dinner is ready," Lisa said. I sat down at the table. He hurried down the stairs and declared, "I am going out, and left." What's wrong with him? I asked Lisa? She replied, "No, not again, he can be stubborn at times, he does that when he's bothered. Don't pay him any attention he can be very sweet but just as sour. I just ignore him." Later in the evening he hasn't returned home yet. I worry if the situation with what Windy Rowe at Lastview implied bothered him so much that he'll stay away. I fell asleep later that night to find him lying next to me awake on his back staring at the ceiling. Anxious, I spoke. "Why did you leave? "I once warned her, Rema Jean, not to go there again. That if she did and was arrested. I couldn't help her next time. Go where? I wish not to think about it anymore. Relax and sleep, we have to be in court tomorrow morning." That night I did just the opposite, unable to sleep, thinking about Barron and this woman. No not again. Did he have some sort of odd affair with her? Like Brittany and Samuel. I think I'll leave the circumstances alone. I've conclude that this is too similar to the situation of Brittany involved with Samuel. Only D.A. Barron was involved with her in some way. If she wasn't in prison her fate could have been the same as the women who that man fatally shot accused of prostitution.

"Good morning Teal", he arose from the bed uttering, "Court this morning the sleeping beauty." Then he went into the bathroom and turned on the music, The Sleeping Beauty by Tchaikovsky, as he showered. I'm feeling sick. No Not Again! So I get out of bed, and hurried to the other bathroom across the hall. I got sick and thought in a couple of hours we'll have court. I'll need something as I staggered off to the kitchen to get some milk to calm my stomach.

Lisa said, "Good morning, Mrs. Adams." Hello mommy," said Brent as he sat at the table eating cereal and watching cartoons. Lisa prepares us breakfast before Brent's day at school, and our day at work. Finally Barron has joined us.

"Good morning Lisa," he said. She continued cooking.

"Yes, my bacon and eggs cooked over medium perfect. Teal I hope to see you in the courtroom." I replied, "I'm not feeling well. I am so under the weather lately. Hoping I can make it to court boss."

"Displeased he demanded well if I'm the boss get a doctor's note. I'll eat breakfast out Lisa." So you're going to leave your breakfast like you left dinner asked Lisa? "Goodbye Lisa." No, not again he has taken offense and left. That morning I couldn't make it to court only to get a doctor's note at his request. The results are three months pregnant. The doctor said, "Congratulations Teal I'll prescribe some vitamins for you and the baby." No not again. I am pregnant with the marriage and move I'd forgotten about the period.

Chapter 8
After The Rain

With a trip in the rain. Right away I must talk to someone other than Barron. So I hurried to see Tasha at the Dott. "I think that is wonderful Teal! I whispered, "I'm not ready to have another baby Tasha, this is private keep your voice down." He's a good man Teal, and you married him, she replied. Meanwhile I looked around, and the others including Oren were staring at me in the Dott.

I screamed "What are you all looking at?"

Rushing out of the restaurant with Oren following behind me.

"Teal what's wrong?"

"What do you want?"

"To see how you're doing?"

"Didn't you hear Tasha, while you and the others scrutinized me?"

"No I have no ideal I didn't hear her, "uttered Oren.

"I feel awful like I've been there before!"

"I'm having a baby, and I am scared."

"I'm sorry, don't be unhappy, remain happy. I quite don't understand the situation with Brittany while she was tough, and stubborn at times, but I can't forget this happened and she's gone. I loved her so much, but I have to forgive you and move on. Sometimes I feel like everybody else has forgotten about her they don't talk about it." I cried, "No, I'll never forget about her. I blame myself and are so sorry."

"Teal I really do care about you, and I am letting go of the anger. So, take a break, I'll pick Brent up he'll stay overnight." I pictured this for the future this is what I wanted to talk about, pleading how sorry I was for not telling him about her and Sam.

So, we continued our conversation in the rain, standing under a rooftop, near the Dott. Gladly we talked about the moment I've dreamed of that finally is here. Those dreams of Brittany that I always have had, because she's always with me I won't ever forget or let her go. I thanked him, and pleaded for forgiveness. I was wrong, it wasn't right for us to go there, and how I wish I could turn the time back. He said sorry I pushed you, and he's here now if I need him. Afterward we embraced in a hug.

I arrived home that rainy afternoon to find Barron sitting at the piano listening to Water Music. Playing a couple of the black and white keys he asked? "Where have you been? Where's Brent?" Exhausted I replied, "I've been at the Dott. Brent's staying with Oren. Barron you left again without eating. So, I must spoil your plans."

He replied, "No."

As he walked up behind me with a hug stating, "You're soaked and smell like men's cologne."

"Well there's a lot of men there and I'm tired also needing to sleep."

"What did the doctor say? "Just nausea." I replied.

That night I'm restless and sobbing as Barron enters the bed whispering, "The rain has stopped now. Why are you crying? Wait let me dry your tears." Currently, he is stroking my body. I felt disgusted and resisted him being pregnant. For I know how aggressive he can be in bed. Sensitive I sobbed. He asked again. "Why are you crying? I'm just tired and want to go back to work. "Don't worry about it Teal. Tomorrow is another day. Get some sleep. Early tomorrow my mother, the newspaper press, and photographer, also the campaign manager along with a few campaign members will be joining us. Leo will cover for you at Lastview until the afternoon. So, let's make it a bright new day."

In the morning, after the rain, I arose early to get in a warm shower. The attire for the day is a beautiful rose-pink suit, styling my hair brushed straight to the back, lifted off my neck in a French braid. A gaze in the mirror, and I was sure this is a good impression for the newspaper press representing Barron's political campaign for Governor. The press will be taking photos as he answers their questions.

"You look stunning Teal." Barron, you love to walk up behind me," I uttered as he gave me a big bear hug, we both gazed at each other in the mirror.

I stated, "You smell great and look handsome." He was wearing a black ensemble, burgundy dress shirt, and a rose, white striped colored tie to accent his suit. "Smile, D.A. Barron," The photographer said. "Can I get a picture of you with your wife, then mother, finally the campaign team?" They shouted. "Next Governor! Barron Adams!"

Meanwhile, Lisa and the others prepared a small breakfast brunch of flavor assorted bagels, donuts, coffee, tea, and water for everybody who attended. Eight months until the big Election Day and I'll tell Barron tonight that I'm expecting, as I feel a little morning sickness. Finally, after everyone left, I snuck into the kitchen for good old-fashioned saltine crackers.

"Teal!"

"Lisa you startled me. I was just..." She asked.

"Teal it isn't any of my business but are you expecting?"

"Lisa please don't tell Barron, I've decided to do that tonight."

Excited he walked into the kitchen and said, "That was fun! Thank goodness it didn't rain again, but it might later. My Mom left. She's going home to sleep it off. She got what she wanted, her son to run for Governor. I'll go to work to complete a couple of things. Wishing Brent, my cartoon partner, was here. When will he be back?" I hurried to the bathroom because the morning sickness was becoming greater as I tried to resist. "Teal, where are you going? What's wrong with her, Lisa? "I don't know I guess she's feeling sick again." Curious, he followed me to the bathroom. Next he opened the door. "No, Barron.

Don't come in here." Teal, are you pregnant? I took a deep breath and said, "Yes, I was going to tell you at dinner tonight, but now you know. Look at me my suit is a mess."

He exclaimed, "Wow! This is great news! Let me help you get into bed." Helping me out of the bathroom. We walked up to the bedroom. Get in the bed. "No Barron I don't want..." He interfered, "You're having my baby. You are sick. Lie down and take the day off." I replied, "No I have to work." He mentioned no, "Leo can cover for you today I'll come back to help you shortly. The task will be short today, after I depose a witness for a case."

That day I stayed in bed, falling to sleep into the late afternoon.

Awakening to Barron whispering. "Teal, my wish came true. Look who's here, and I brought dinner home." Burgers and fries. "I'm back mom! "Brent, I miss you! Soon you'll be a big brother. In the meantime, let us go get ice cream." I jumped out of the bed. "Hold on. Slow down Teal, said Barron. How are you feeling? I responded, burgers, fries and vanilla, chocolate, or strawberry ice cream. Brent's response, "fudge swirl ice cream."

Barron's response, "superman ice cream then up and away I go to bed I'm exhausted." That night I read a book to Brent until he had fallen asleep. The day worked out for the best, with the campaign event and Brent returning home. Tomorrow I will make it back to work at Lastview.

Back to work, the days, weeks, and months go by. Sitting here six months into my pregnancy. The inmates are keeping the place clean and the flowers are well planted and taken care of in between the rain. The prisoners are now demanding results of the reviews that I have already conducted. "It's been slow with the parole board." Leo exclaimed, "Warden Teal we have a problem. The inmate Windy Rowe is complaining again." I said, "Have them bring her down. Is there a problem Windy? She said, "I want out of here! It's been three months now. I deserve another review, but oh I heard you was on his side. Well you tell him I have children too." With empathy I expressed, "Ok Windy I'll work on it." Anxiety was starting to overwhelm me. "Leo I can't deal with her complaints, D.A. Barron needs to address this situation." While she waited right away I called his business phone he didn't answer. "Have the men take her back to her cell. I have to go to the court and talk to him." Leo replied, "Windy Rowe thinks that she is special. I think you shouldn't go leave it up to the parole board."

"She is special, and won't give up, I hear it in her voice. I'll take it to D.A. Barron.

This needs his immediate attention."

The D.A.'s Deputy asked, "Can I help you, Mrs. Adams? Oh, thank goodness."

"Where's D.A. Adams? "He's in court. Maybe you should sit down until he's finished; you look like you're going in any day now." He's right so I sat and waited, but it took some time, and I was getting impatient. I'll peak in. There he was, sitting in the courtroom with a female judge. They looked as they're enjoying each other's company. This clearly explains why he wasn't answering his phone. With feelings of envy, I left and returned home. I called him again, he didn't answer his phone.

Later that evening he arrived home and asked. "How are you feeling? My assistant said you were at the court. "I was worried about the inmate Windy Rowe. She wants another review, the other reviews didn't pass, so Barron I suspect she's right. It's been sometime and I think this one needs your immediate attention." He walked amongst Teal whispering in her ear, "Not all reviews pass." What is your notion then? D.A. Barron exclaimed, "What is my notion? Teal, since you want to change things I motion for you to take maternity leave. I think you're putting more on your plate than you can digest."

"What do you mean?"

"Well, you leave work to look for me, not to mention calling my phone while I'm in court. Overall, you aren't following protocol of the laws applied. The rules don't change, and there is no exception for inmates." I screamed, "Even if she's under stress and has a family! The stupid record for being a stripper, I call it a mistake! Why are you holding these women like that?"

"Stripper turned prostitutes I can't control it. Sometimes the laws help protect others more, rather than hurt them. Think about it, if they were still on the streets, it might've been them that suffered, like the same two women, who were killed by the man, who suffered by your hands, but I don't want to go there." Don't you dare do it, because I confided in you, so now you think I'm proud of what I did? "Well the truth hurts. So, stay in your place and concentrate on the baby, and the Bar exam I'll help you study, but to the point I insist you take maternity leave at the end of the month." Standing there in shock. I thought, he is right; as much as I try to think he's wrong. "That lady, Windy. What will happen to her?

"She'll be transferred out of Lastview prison."

"No Barron, she doesn't have much time left."

"Teal, you cannot change this! I can't change the sentence the judge gave them! She'll finish it somewhere else. Goodnight, I'm exhausted." The D.A. lay down and thought, frankly I'm sick of hearing about this Windy. She doesn't know the truth and that Rema. She's a liar. I never should have gone to that place. Despite all that makeup she wore. I couldn't take my eyes off her that night. Then the money I spent on her in there. Not to mention later, it'll become a crime scene. I might be a nice guy, but I'm not a pushover.

Chapter 9
The Test

Finally. I'm here taking the Bar examination at the test site, reminiscing about when Barron helped me with these questions. The D.A. asked number one?

"List the four Justifiability doctrines?" I answered, "Standing, ripeness, mootness, political question."

"Correct Teal," he uttered. "Thank you, future Governor. Next question?"

"List four exceptions to the Miranda requirement? You should know this, you're an ex- cop."

"Routine booking questions, jailhouse informants, undercover agents, public safety."

"That's right Teal. How about this question? What is the meaning of the word Statute?

"A law made recorded in formal document." I don't think the D.A. expected to ask this next question because, I remembered at the time he looked down at the book, and was reading it with his eyes, and I said, "Come on, keep it going."

What is the hearsay exception? Before I could answer he handed me the book, kissed me on the forehead and mumbled. "You're doing a great job." Looking down at the answers I'm reminded. Exception of hearsay means relating to a startling event that is made while the declarant was under stress, or excitement caused by an event or condition. At the time I thought he was thinking about Rema and Windy. Did the two play the declarant to him or me? They are under great stress about being in jail, however I sit and think that, I could've been the declarant when I saw Brittany with Samuel if I would've informed the department she wouldn't be gone, however the women, Rema Jean and Windy Rowe, were spared because of the laws.

Suddenly I finished, arose, and handed my book to the instructor. The exam lasted the whole day. When I arrived home later that evening Barron was in bed reading a book about raising babies. I remark, "I see you're looking forward to the baby."

"Yes I am. How did the exam go?"

"Fine but I'm exhausted."

"Sure, you are," he responded. "Good night."

"Teal, Teal! Wake up! What the? Why is it wet? Barely awake I said, "I don't know Barron. I think my water broke." He replied, "The baby is coming are you, all right?"

"I have to go to the hospital. Get the bag while I get dressed. Brent will have to come along. I'll call Tasha to meet us there."

Tasha said, "I'm here Teal. Breathe! Where is that doctor?"

"Oh, it hurts!" I yelled.

"Three short breaths at a time, Barron replied."

"The doctor finally entered the room and asked, "Teal, are you ready? Yes. Time to push. Congratulations, it's a boy!"

The doctor said, "Do you want to cut the umbilical cord, dad? Yes, and his name will be Barron Adams the second." Tasha commented, "He's beautiful." Brent joined us and said, "I have a baby brother." Yes, I thought he looked like Barron with the straight black hair weighing eight pounds.

After midnight, well into the dawn of the day, Barron's mom visited the hospital with the Governor's wife and daughter, accompanied by the fresh smell of freshly picked carnations they brought along, to see the baby. Presenting the flowers, they were all proud as they looked on.

The D.A. exclaimed again, his name is Barron the second. His mom expressed, "Just in time for the election." The Governor's wife stated, "two months left, and we'll be leaving the mansion, moving to the island, with the Governor relieved of his duty."

"I, if I'm lucky enough to win, D.A Barron said."

All laughed with excitement. The nurse walked in and said, "Feeding time."

"We'll be leaving now. Good day. I love my grandson."

"The D.A said I think I should also leave a s well. I'm not used to this sort of thing." The nurse recommended, "You should learn how to use the bottle, dad."

"Teal, aren't you going to nurse the baby? I read in the baby book, that it's best for the baby, and I believe the directions in the book." The nurse responded, "I'll leave the bottle here, and let you all figure it out." I thought about work and nursing the baby. The D.A. wanted to help. He said, "Look, the baby is doing a good job at it."

"Wait a minute, Barron! Just let me try the bottle."

"Wail, Wail!" the baby cried.

"Teal, nursing the baby is the best."

"Ok Barron!"

Sitting there feeding this baby I thought, I'm starting over with a newborn baby however, I have to get back to work at Lastview.

It has been a month now. Therefore, it is closer to election time. Just a few weeks left, and I've been staying at home taking care of the baby. "Lisa, on Saturday can you come in and babysit for Barron? Brent will stay with Oren, I would like to surprise Barron and give myself a beauty treatment, before the election since it's coming up soon."

"So, can you watch him?"

"Which Barron, the first or the second?"

"Lisa, the second. Don't mention it to Barron. I'd prefer that he'd play golf. Especially because it's his day off." She said, "I understand and will be happy to do it." "Good Saturday morning, D.A. Barron," said Lisa.

"Good morning. What are you doing here? Where's Teal and Brently at? "They went out, and I'm babysitting so...Would you like some breakfast? Barron the second is sleeping."

"No but I'd like if you enjoyed your day off. I can

watch over my own son. I can't believe Teal snuck out of here and didn't tell me."

"Well, today you play golf, and she made a request for me here to babysit, so I informed her I would be happy to do it." He replied, "For your information, it's my baby, and I'm the boss take the day off."

With disappointment Lisa said, "Right you're the boss, so I think you should call and inform her you are going to do it. I don't want to argue about it I'm leaving. Remember she's breast feeding so his bottle is right here. Have patience!"

The beauty therapist said, "Lay back and relax. This will not hurt you at all."

She massaged my feet. Then performed a pedicure on my toes I've fallen to sleep.

The dream I had Oren screaming!

"What happened Teal?"

"Why are the two of you here? Dreaming about the time Brittany was laid to rest. The service had ended. "Oren, Oren I'm so sorry." He replied, "I don't want to ever speak about it again, it's over I just want to be left alone." That same day I revealed to Oren that I was expecting and, I had to protect our baby. His mouth shook as he kissed me on the lips whispering, "I will be there for our baby."

Then he walked away.

"Wail, Wail," the baby cried. "Please take your bottle. He won't stop crying. I'll call your mom. Ring, Ring, she's not answering her phone. I'll try her business phone. Wait a minute I hear it."

Jingle, Jingle. "That's her business phone jingling. Damn she left it here! Finally the baby has cried himself to sleep.

The therapist said, "Mrs. Adams, Mrs. Adams I'm finished. How do you like it?"

I awoke, I love it. The make-up accents are beautiful colors also my finger nails, and toenails are painted in a very beautiful lively color and all. "Thank you, I cannot believe I fell asleep, lately I've been so exhausted. Really, the first break I have had in a while with a new baby also the election is coming up."
She replied, "Well tell Mr. Adams he has my vote."

Finally arriving to the house. "I'm home, Lisa.

"How did he do with the bottle?"

"He cried the whole time. Why didn't you tell me you were leaving this morning?"

"Barron you surprised me. I went out for a beauty

treatment and wanted to surprise you. Look at my make-up. Where's Lisa?"

"I sent her home. I tried to call you, and I hear Jingling. You left your business phone here, and that's not good."

I replied, "Sorry, I fell asleep and I didn't know our baby was business. Guess that's what happens when you mix business with pleasure. So I guess since you're the boss. You only listen to your side of the story. Anyway you have done the same thing." "No, Teal I'll remind you, I was working my ass off, not sneaking out to get even with you, and you look like a whore with all that make-up on your face."

"What did you say? Did you call me a whore?"

"Yes, I did, and it doesn't turn me on."

"Well what does it do then intimidate you?"

"Barron I wasn't being sneaky exhausted I fell asleep. Then I had a dream about Brittany again somewhere I must be under some pressure," "Well I suggest you need to let Brittany go." "Like you did them women at Lastview? You didn't let them go, only moving them." He responded. "Why must we go over this again? Let them go where back on the streets?"

"Just don't ever tell me, to let Brittany go with your cold self!"

"I don't know who's colder, Teal; me or you."

"What do you mean by that Barron?"

"When I think more about it, you really did let her go, and could have avoided that shooting, keeping her out of the hands of that gangster. Do you ever dream about that? Maybe you should, it might make you feel better."

"So I'm on trial now? I guess you forgot about that convict, because I did your dirty work for you, and pulled the trigger. While you stood there looking around like Mr. Perfect. I saved you from an emotional experience." He replied, "I call it self-defense, but you're right, the dirty part of the law applied. It was just in the Courtroom with that convict, and the men dead on the street, not at Lastview perfect timing, "He said as he gathered his golf equipment. Devastated I asked. What will you do if it happened to you? "You're a coward, Barron! It makes me sick you can't even face them women and tell the truth looking for an excuse. You couldn't handle it, and pull the switch, of the results in this most difficult occupation Love, Lost, Lastview!"

Shocked, he said, "Now we really know how each other feels."

"Wail, Wail the baby cries."

"I'll just go get our son now." When I returned he left, I can hear him in his car speed away.

On his arrival to play golf he imagined, time for me now, to make at least, three good shots as quick as I can. Upon arriving the caddy asked, "What's the goal today?" He said, "Shoot at least three golf balls, quickly in the holes, with the least amount of swings. See how it feels to get even." Successful he is. "You did it!" Expressed the caddy.

"Yes!" The District Attorney states, and he is happy yet thinking he has hurt Teal.

After arriving home, Barron entered the bed. "Sleeping beauty, I love your hair, makeup, and nails. You did this for me. Thank you I don't expect you to forget about what happened to Brittany. Sorry I feel, it hurt you, for me to say such things. He sucked on my toes and whispered, I want you so bad."

"Barron you have to ease up. I can't do it now. I care about Windy and Rema. The stylist said she will vote for you. When I first started the job at Lastview, you told me not to be gullible. I'm convinced that you should let them women go, and I accept your apology." He whispered, "shhh let's not ruin the moment from now on it's my business. Goodnight."

Chapter 10
Drum Roll

"Hello, Newspaper press this is Rema Jean I have some news for you. It's about the D.A. Barron Adams, running for Governor. I'm in jail because of the very spot he came to see me at the Gentlemen's Club. That is why he has me in this prison. He wants everyone to think he's perfect." The guard ordered, "Rema Jean hang that phone up right now!" Laughing she said, "I just had to make an important phone call ha ha ha!"

"Barron, I passed the Bar exam!" Sitting down in the chair, holding the newspaper, Barron was sad expressing, "I tried to cover it up." The newspaper stated, "The Candidate for Governor, D.A. Barron, said to be seen mingling with strippers at the Gentlemen's Club."

"Teal, maybe you were right." Ring, ring. Lisa answered the phone. "D.A. Barron, it's your mom." Disappointed he said, "What mother I'm listening?"

The Governor and his wife are present with her, as she addresses him over the phone.

"Did you see the newspaper?"

"Yes mother."

"Is it true? Did you go there?"

"Yes a long time ago, when we first arrived to this town." She nodded her head. The Governor laughed and whispered, "I didn't think he had it in him, and I can't believe he's married now either, it isn't a big deal." The Governor's wife said, "Silence, it's not funny. He's an important person."

"I thought I, and your father taught you, self-respect, and determination to be the best; to finally run for office. Well I'm embarrassed to be your mother. You were an important person. Now you're just like the others. Frustrated she said, "How could you be caught in a place like that?"

"Did you solicit her for sex?"

"No mother, I swear on the Bible."

"I'm still embarrassed she said, "The campaign manager and I will set up a newspaper press conference very early tomorrow morning. So you can inform them that you stepped out of your comfort zone visiting that place."

The D.A. screamed, "Mother, whose life is it anyway! You think this job is a walk in the park?" "No, but unfortunately it has come to this. Maybe losing your career, and the race for Governor. Fix it and, plead the 1st amendment's freedom of association for being in such a place."

"Mother, I didn't touch her." She responded, "But you went there." Then she hung up the phone. Furious, D.A. Barron threw the phone he was using on the floor, and it broke into pieces!

Lisa returned to the room and said, "The baby is asleep. Why did you do that?"

"Not now Lisa!" He shouted. Insulted Lisa leaves.

"Barron just tell me what happened? What's bothering you?"

"I guess I lost my composure now. Then starting this prestigious job as the District Attorney. The first week in this big house is lonely; nobody here but me, I was bored. So new to the town, I felt for a moment I wanted to be like everyone else riding around listening to the music, enjoying the beautiful weather. A warm calm night it was, I saw this place and it looked harmless. So I decided to give it a try. After ordering a few drinks I noticed nothing but men were there, except for the waitresses. The music started as I was captivated by the beat then their lights dimmed, except on the dance floor. Next an announcement, "Meet Rema Jean! "The other men were clapping. Then I thought this is a Gentlemen's' Club. I better get out of here fast; however when she came out I was struck by her beauty, and sort of turned on by her perfect body, and beautiful hair. She noticed I was infatuated. So I drank and enjoyed her dancing like everybody else. The closer she got to me she wore so much makeup.

"Thank you for the two hundred dollars she said."

"You're welcome. Here's another two hundred."

"Thank you gorgeous, can I dance for you?"

"So she danced for me, whispering in my ear
        for five hundred dollars, you can have it all."

I replied, "No, not with all that makeup on your face, it doesn't turn me on. So she told me to go play with myself.

Then I stood up and left. Six months later the deputy assistant phoned me that he was going to be late for court. He asked, "Can I take the first-time charges for the prostitute? I told him yes, it was for her, the stripper Rema Jean. There she was sitting in the conference room I went in too."

She uttered, "Oh my goodness, it's you."

"Well yes, now I really know the truth, you're capable of soliciting yourself for money remember, but I'm going to let you off this time, as a first-time offender, dismissing the charges. Don't go back to that place. If you do, I'll have to protect the civil rights of the other woman who work at that club just to dance. Don't make it hard for those girls, just there, doing their job dancing." She replied, "I won't ever go back to that place again. Then sign your name right here next to mine. Your Honor, the defendant, Rema Jean, has signed a formal statement that she will never go back to that place again. So, the state's request is to dismiss the charges. Request granted." The judge declared. The next time I viewed her, she was in court again and, the deputy attorney was there to take his own case. Out of my hands. She was sentenced to two years for prostitution, with time off for good behavior by the judge. The incident when she spit in my face added two more years to her sentence. Four years all together. My signature accept I never touched her, Teal. My mother wants me to plead the first amendment for association. Somewhere I think she wanted me to be her keeper, and I warned her not go back there again, getting her off the first time. The next time no special favors as a result with all the complaints of her sounding off, the bitch sounded off to the newspaper. Maybe I should've listened to you, and let her go, but the law is the law. Now I wish I would've never added on that time and released her."

"Barron it's not a big deal you're human, and we all make mistakes. I want you to relax then go for a swim. Put this behind you until tomorrow."

He said, "The campaign will call for a newspaper press conference in the morning. Great, just tell the newspapers the truth, by informing them that she was just a convict that wanted special favors. In the meantime, the baby is sleeping, and Lisa isn't here." He said, "I forgot about Lisa I didn't mean to scream at her."

"It's all right now, let's listen to the peaceful, and quiet atmosphere, celebrate the passing of the exam with some wine, lighting the candles. Then sit by the pool. "You're right Teal. Congratulations, I won't let it spoil you passing the exam."

"Good, I'll be back in twenty minutes."

So Teal took a deep breath, then showered, and

put on a white lingerie. Approaching the swimming pool. There is Barron sobbing, sitting at the bar, by the pool surrounded with the candles burning heavily drinking, and smoking a cigar. Then he arose and dived in the pool swimming the first lap, then another lap back. Finally finished, meeting Teal at the end of the swimming pool. He jumped out, grabbed his towel, and approached Teal. "Barron I'm ready, she said." Quickly he wiped his face then the rest of his body dry, he lay the towel down, and Teal on the floor right in front of the pool. Eagerly he kissed her while he's slowly taking the lingerie off her body. He is anxious to absorb her breast with his mouth again, opening her legs, headed between her thighs. Then the injection of his hard man piece penetrated up inside of her filling Teal up, releasing all Barron had in him to the very last drop. He is so aggressive with maximum arousal, she cried out, "Barron, Barron! He replied, "Teal I really needed this love." Then they are finished and exhausted, as both of them retired to bed. He lay close to her and uttered, "What a day." Then they both fall quietly sound to sleep.

Very early that quiet morning he woke up with feelings of discouragement, and attended to the baby awake, and a call from his campaign manager. Hello, how are you sir? "Disappointed with the whole ordeal, I feel like my life is crumbling before me but I'm hanging in there." The meeting will take place at the lobby of the Newspaper Press Department in one hour. I remind you with solidarity the campaign has your back 100%. We're still in the race." Humbled, the D.A. replied, "I will see you there. Thank you."

Holding the babbling baby, he expressed, "Daddy has to go. I have to make this right for you, and the people who trust me. Teal, I need you to take the baby. I'm leaving to give a statement to the newspaper press, and I'll be back shortly."

"Good luck Barron, stay calm, and be strong."

Next he went to the kitchen expecting coffee to be made by Lisa, but she was not there. Then the D.A. opened his closet, and took out his suit admiring the way Lisa kept his outfits together.

He treasured, Lisa my friend, I didn't mean to raise my voice at you. Then he tuned into it again, the song Water Music by Handel, entering the shower. The tears fell once more, but he knew as the steamy hot water sprayed his face, he had to regain his composure.

Finally finished in the shower he dried himself, turned the music off, and then looked in the mirror, thinking that it was his duty to gain his self-control. Then he dressed in his suit, and off to the meeting he went.

The press reporter was present, as well as his campaign manager and his mother. Others didn't attend for reasons that it was just an implication of Barron being in that place. Apparently, he was a strong example running for the office of Governor.

"District Attorney Adams, can you give us an explanation about the call to the paper regarding your association with that stripper Rema Jean who claimed you attended the Gentlemen's Club? Asked the reporter. Regarding the incidents that have taken place outside the establishment. Do you believe it was in bad taste to go there D.A Barron?"

He declared, "Yes, five years ago I saw that women Rema Jean dance, but just only a quick view. Only for her to be placed in detention at Lastview, I, D.A. Barron Adams's only concern has been to respect, protect, work, and defend the public in and out of the courtroom. I'm happily married now with a son. The newspaper spoke of me in one sentence. "The candidate for Governor, D.A. Barron said to have attended the Gentlemen's club." Now for my statement in one sentence. "Please don't dramatize these accusations without the facts. Have a wonderful morning. Thank you." His mother said, "Great job, Barron. Now I know you better. You have spoken, and I'm not embarrassed but happy that your father, and I taught you how to stay confident.

District Attorney Barron's Election Day celebration is presently at his home. His supporters shouted, "Governor, Governor!" Holding signs, wearing buttons pinned to their shirts reading, "D.A. Barron for Governor." The others shouted along with the supporters, holding bright colored red, white, and blue balloons including, the assistant District Attorney, Chief of police, Lisa, his mother, Tasha, her daughter Angela, Brently, and the residing Governor with his wife and daughter at his side.

At the time D.A. Barron was holding Barron the second in his arms. Teal observed. They really think he's a winner. "One more hour until we'll know the results," the campaign manager announced.

"While the D.A. humbled himself, literally thanking all that supported, and helped him by reminding them of his civil duty."

"Hold on the outcome is," Said the campaign manager."

Everyone becomes silent. "The D.A. would not be performing the job."

One interrupted, "No I can't believe it."

Another mumbled, "He didn't make it."

Lisa stumbled into the room and said, "Are you serious?" The secretary said, "you're stuck with me."

Individuals present in the room grumbled, looking at the D.A. as he held the baby close to him. Shocked, he took a breath and immediately responded, "I acknowledge all of you that have joined, and worked on the campaign."

The campaign manager exclaimed, "Wait a minute! Drum roll! It is my pleasure, and I'm sure everyone will agree. You won't be performing the job as the District Attorney any longer."

"Congratulations you were elected as our new Governor!" The D.A. looked on astonished with a smile, and was very pleased. He announced, "I owe it to all of you solemnly, to do the best civil duty as your Governor. Now let's celebrate. Continue to eat, and drink. Caps off the champagne. Enjoy the music. Badinerie by Bach. Thank you for your support!"

He has won, and the election is over. Governor Barron Adams is pleased with the results, and Teal is back to work at Lastview looking forward to a future in practicing Civil Law. Time has passed, and Barron has taken his position as the Governor. They reside along, with the flowers in the Governor's mansion. The former Governor has moved his family to the Island. Teal suffered the loss of Brittany. She'll never be forgotten. She wondered if it was a way to love again, in the midst of this most dangerous occupation, and it was. She is content as Warden of Lastview. Everyone else has moved on with their lives. Sitting there in her office at the prison. Jingle, jingle! The business phone rings. It's Barron. "Teal I have news, on some reviews. You should find this interesting that I, the residing Governor now, have the power. So it's an early release, this sunny early morning for Rema Jean and Windy Rowe." Teal responded, "Well all is good here at the facility to. The prison is clean with the fresh smell of pine, and the inmates are taking care of the flowers, shrubs, trees, and bushes here at LASTVIEW."

THE END

ABOUT THE AUTHOR

"My name is Candace Taylor Johnson. I am a new Author. My first Novel is Nella A Ballpark Worker Book I. My hobbies are human service, classical movies, music, reading, animals, and sports. A Violinist since the age of eight years old I enjoy melodies, tempos, and harmonies creative arts in that place literally expressing the novel. So, I write KnackTime Writings, born in Anderson Indiana I reside in Michigan now. The State of the Great Lakes. In the future I'll write books rich enough for you to experience. The art of fiction and non-fiction literature. Enjoy Lastview. For me it is my masterpiece literature. A novel about Love, Lost and Lastview Prison."

Coming Soon From KnackTime Books:

Nella A Novella Day Book II
(Literary fiction)

"Sharkey Street, Where I Am From, A True Story."
(Geography Non-Fiction)

I invite you my readers to my official twitter
account: @KnackTime

The Facebook page, home to Lastview for the music
literally expressed in the novel and comments.
http://www.facebook.com/viewLastview

Thank You And I Appreciate Your Reading
KnackTime Books.